Pretty Is

Pretty Is

Elizabeth Holmes

DUTTON CHILDREN'S BOOKS

DUTTON CHILDREN'S BOOKS
A division of Penguin Young Readers Group

Published by the Penguin Group
Penguin Group (USA) Inc., 375 Hudson Street, New York, New York 10014, U.S.A. •
Penguin Group (Canada), 90 Eglinton Avenue East, Suite 700, Toronto, Ontario, Canada
M4P 2Y3 (a division of Pearson Penguin Canada Inc.) • Penguin Books Ltd, 80 Strand,
London WC2R 0RL, England • Penguin Ireland, 25 St Stephen's Green, Dublin 2, Ireland
(a division of Penguin Books Ltd) • Penguin Group (Australia), 250 Camberwell Road,
Camberwell, Victoria 3124, Australia (a division of Pearson Australia Group Pty Ltd) • Penguin
Books India Pvt Ltd, 11 Community Centre, Panchsheel Park, New Delhi – 110 017, India •
Penguin Group (NZ), 67 Apollo Drive, Mairangi Bay, Auckland 1311, New Zealand
(a division of Pearson New Zealand Ltd) • Penguin Books (South Africa) (Pty) Ltd,
24 Sturdee Avenue, Rosebank, Johannesburg 2196, South Africa

Penguin Books Ltd, Registered Offices: 80 Strand, London WC2R 0RL, England

CIP Data is available.

Published in the United States by Dutton Children's Books,
a division of Penguin Young Readers Group
345 Hudson Street, New York, New York 10014
www.penguin.com/youngreaders

Designed by Beth Herzog

Printed in USA   First Edition

10 9 8 7 6 5 4 3 2 1   ISBN 978-0-525-47813-3

For my brother, Robert,
and in memory of my sister, Mary

ACKNOWLEDGMENTS

Thanks to three of the best readers and writers I've ever known—Paul Cody, Martha Collins, and Brian Hall—as well as young readers Liam and Austin Cody and Madeleine Moss for their advice and encouragement. And thanks to my extraordinary agent, Sara Crowe; my skillful editor, Lucia Monfried; and all the people at Dutton for transforming 344 kilobytes of text into that everyday miracle, a real live between-covers hold-in-your-hands book.

Contents

Pretty Is

Chapter 1

A Bad Feeling

I am Frodo; I carry the Ring.

It rests in my pocket, powerful and secret. Only I know it's there. I look small and ordinary, but I have strength and dignity and more courage than anyone would ever guess.

I carry myself straight, arms folded across my chest. Around me the villagers go chattering about their business—thoughtless, knowing nothing of the danger, nothing of who I am.

I find myself in a room with a circle of chairs: the Council of Elrond. There's argument all around me, but in a moment my voice will silence them all. My voice, firm and clear: "I will take the Ring."

But instead I heard another firm, clear voice—"Take your seat, Erin"—and it was like I'd been on a long plane ride and my ears had finally popped. Mrs. Winsted, my teacher. Fifth grade. A circle of desks, and I was standing just outside it, still holding my backpack. Everyone else sitting down, their things put away, looking at me.

I slunk into my seat, not Frodo of the Shire anymore, just plain Erin, caught daydreaming again. Now Mrs. Winsted would probably tell Mama—again—that I didn't pay attention.

I slid my backpack under my desk, then glanced hastily around the room to see if anyone was still staring at me. Most of the kids, I saw with relief, had gone back to flipping through their notebooks or whispering to each other or gazing out the window; only Ricky Talmadge was giving me a puzzled look. Hannah McLaren caught my eye and grinned as if we were sharing a terrific joke, and suddenly I felt better. Hannah could do that—could make you feel like things were fine, without saying a word. She had this grin that somehow said, *Who cares? It's funny—we're all funny!*

Mrs. Winsted's heels went clicking around the circle behind me, and I straightened up and tried to listen as the loudspeaker crackled on and the principal, grouchy old Mr. Stimson, read the morning announcements in his gravelly voice: Academic Fun Night this Thursday, bring in your pledges for the Readathon, no climbing on the wall beside the playground.

As soon as he was done, Mrs. Winsted started talking about the tour of J. B. Marsh Middle School that she'd planned for next week. As usual, she paced around the room while she talked, as if she had too much energy to stand still. "Permission slips went home yesterday," she reminded us. "I only got six or seven back this morning. The rest of you better get those in before Wednesday—signed by a parent—or you'll be sitting here going boo-hoo while everybody else gets on the bus."

Then she gave us one of her I-mean-business looks—chin down, eyebrows raised, a brief stare down her nose—that always followed a warning like an exclamation point at the end of a sentence. By this time of year, heading into our last month at Sandy Creek Elementary, we knew for a fact that she did mean business, but we also knew that nobody was going to be left behind.

Mrs. Winsted had a ton of frizzy blond hair and a loud voice. After the last parent-teacher conference, Mama said, "Erin Chaney, it's a mystery to me how anybody could *not* pay attention to Mrs. Winsted."

Around the middle of last fall, when the newness of fifth grade had worn off, I'd started noticing how babyish the kindergartners and first graders were, and how the school assemblies were more for them than for big kids like fifth graders. I was too big for some of the structures on the playground; I was bored with the library and the art room and the gym. By Thanksgiving, and ever since, I'd been eager to get out of Sandy Creek and go on to middle school.

When I woke up this morning, though, I wasn't so sure.

As I lay in bed I heard Mama rattling around in the kitchen, accompanied by the low hum of news on the radio, and some floor creaking followed by a thud that meant Daddy had reached the limit of his morning push-ups. I heard the scrape of coat hangers in my sister's closet, the closing of a drawer. Normally these were cozy sounds, when I was still drowsy, lying in bed with sun streaming in, and no one making me get up.

But today I didn't feel cozy, and middle school didn't sound so wonderful. I woke up thinking about Kayla, who was in my class and sort of a friend of mine, and Kayla's big sister, Claire, and some things that had happened lately. I was caught up in a swirl of thoughts that seemed to have surfaced somewhere in my dreams and carried over, filling my head, awake or asleep. And I started to have this bad feeling about sixth grade.

Mama was calling me to get up. I pushed the feeling away and turned into Frodo, camping with the elves, waking up high in a tree. A breakfast of cold water and *lembas*, the elves' bread, then dressing in my tunic and the magical gray cloak the elves gave me for my journey.

As Frodo I walked to school; as Frodo I did not think any of those swirling thoughts or feel the weight of that bad feeling about sixth grade.

But now, in class, I was only Erin, and as soon as I heard about the middle-school visit, the bad feeling jumped me like a springy trick snake out of a box.

The name of the bad feeling was Monica.

The day before we'd had a soccer match after school, and I'd gone over to Kayla's house after the game. We'd lost, 3–2, and I'd missed a clear shot at the goal.

"No way is that girl in fifth grade," I muttered, up in Kayla's bedroom. I rubbed my ankle where this huge girl on the other team had accidentally-on-purpose tripped me. I'd been griping about her as Kayla's mom was driving us home.

"She's a cow," Kayla said, but without a lot of feeling. She poked a finger around delicately in her jewelry box and pulled out heart-shaped earrings. She'd already changed into blue shorts and a white shirt the minute we got there, but I was still in my sweaty soccer clothes, the shiny shorts and kneesocks and the team T-shirt. Kayla hated to be sweaty.

She didn't even seem to care that we'd lost, and I remembered how at the last practice she'd sat out some of the drills. She told Ms. Ruston, the coach, that her knee hurt, but she told Hannah and me she was bored to tears. She pulled a Walkman out of her backpack and lay back on the grass, listening. The trees next to the soccer field were full of tiny white blossoms and baby leaves the color of Crayola spring green, but Kayla was only looking at sky.

Losing had already made me cranky, and remembering that practice made me cranky toward Kayla. "You don't even try to win," I muttered.

"Yes I do!" Kayla shot a look at me, then looked away,

turning her head aside as she put on the earrings, as if that was the only way she could do it. "Anyway, it's just a game," she said in an oh-so-mature voice. I pretended to be interested in her bulletin board.

It still had lots of pictures she'd drawn the summer before, when we were into drawing these sequences of pictures, almost like stories, of two girls and their horses. Sometimes we drew the horses with ribbons braided into their manes and tails, and sometimes we drew the girls in proper riding clothes, like we'd seen in a book, and then laughed at the funny-looking pants.

The pictures, I thought, should be in a museum. Not because they were good, but because they were old, they were ancient history. Kayla could draw a lot better than me, but she even had a couple of my drawings on the bulletin board, too. Whoever's house we drew them at, that person kept them. Not that Kayla exactly treasured them—she just never cleaned her room. Her bulletin board also had the program from the third-grade play. Which she wasn't even in, except in the chorus.

I still had a lot of the horse pictures in my room, too, but they were in a drawer. I stuffed them in there the first time Kayla said she didn't want to draw together anymore. I got used to that after a while. She wanted to play CDs and look at magazines and do our fingernails in glitter polish. She was my friend for that kind of thing and Hannah was my friend for mancala and Monopoly and soccer, which

Hannah was really good at and definitely wanted to win at all times. But she never liked to draw.

Sometimes I wondered if I was the same Erin with Kayla that I was with Hannah. And did anybody else ever change to be like me, or was I the only one? Like Silly Putty that takes the shape of whatever you put it on.

I was picking up the little china horses on Kayla's dresser one by one, rubbing the dust off their smooth coats, when Kayla's sister, Claire, paused in the doorway, leaning against it. The word *willowy* was invented for Claire.

"Kayla," she said, but Kayla was bent over, brushing her long blond-brown hair upside down, and didn't look up. "Oh, hi, Erin. Kayla, did you take my blue eye shadow?"

The rhythm of the hairbrush paused briefly, then resumed. Kayla always made a big show of brushing her hair for about a hour, it seemed like. What made this especially annoying was that her hair really was gorgeous—long and golden and shimmery.

"Mmm—oh yeah, it's in the bathroom."

"Ever heard of asking?" Lately Claire had developed this slow, offhand voice that didn't necessarily mean she was easygoing.

"No, what's that?"

"Ha-ha," said Claire, turning to go.

"Hey, Claire." Kayla was upright now, pink in the face. "Tell Erin about her sister."

"Monica?" My insides squirmed. Kayla's voice told me this wasn't going to be pleasant.

Claire twirled back toward us on her toes and draped herself in the doorway again. "Oh jeez, this is too funny. You know that new jacket she got?"

I did. It was a cheap, light jacket, a navy-blue windbreaker with snaps in the front. Nothing like the Polartecs or jean jackets or anything else the other girls would wear. Monica's kind of tall and gangly, and the jacket makes her look really dorky.

I hadn't said anything when she brought it home from the mall, or the first time she wore it. Now I wished I'd said "Take it back" about fifty times and rolled my eyes and ridiculed it until she slunk back to the store for a refund. Except it would never have worked. I knew Monica. The more you objected to something she was doing, the more she would keep on doing it.

"Well," Claire went on, "Wesley Brennan noticed the other day that it's exactly like the one Miss McGill wears every day."

I knew Wesley Brennan—tall, cute, played basketball—but I had to ask who Miss McGill was.

"The lunch lady," Kayla put in gleefully, pulling her hair into a ponytail and putting a ribbon around it. "She's about a hundred years old."

"And she talks funny. I think she's like retarded or something," said Claire. "She's like, 'Mash pertaters? You want some mash pertaters?'" She twisted her face into a big-eyed, goofy grin. Kayla giggled.

"Anyway." Claire returned her face to normal and spun around once on her toes like a ballerina, arms in a circle over her head, before continuing. "Wesley's got so much nerve. In the lunch line he's like, 'So Monica, you and Miss McGill got matching clothes, huh? You two going shopping together this weekend?'

"And then Mark Malone goes, 'Hey, Wesley, be sweet to your girlfriend—Monica *likes* you.' And Wesley says the S-word, and Mark goes, 'It's true, man. I have inside information. Girls talk, in case you ain't noticed.' And Monica turned so red, everybody knew it was true, and anyway, I already knew it, 'cause Wendy got it out of her one day and told a whole bunch of us."

Claire rolled her eyes. "Can you imagine *Monica* with Wesley Brennan? Everybody in the whole line was laughing, and some of the boys started saying 'Wooooh' and 'She wants you, Wesley' and stuff like that. She was red as fire, and Wesley got embarrassed too, and he kept saying the S-word till a couple of teachers came over and told everybody to settle down."

Claire and Kayla were both looking at me, waiting for my reaction.

I felt my face go hot and red under their stares, and I couldn't think of a thing to say. Finally I muttered weakly, "Yeah, that jacket is really dorky."

"For *real*," Kayla crowed.

Claire giggled. "I bet she and Miss McGill go down to the Goodwill store every Saturday. Miss McGill gets herself a couple of those old-lady housedresses—"

"And Monica gets some fluffy white knee socks," put in Kayla.

"And a hairnet like Miss McGill's—"

They went on and on. Kayla kept shooting these sharp little glances at me, like she wanted to see me squirm.

I grinned, and hated myself for grinning.

I felt about five or six things at once—mad at all those kids for laughing at Monica, ashamed of being Monica's sister, mad at Monica for being such a dork, ashamed of not knowing what to say. Maybe most of all I felt mad at Claire and Kayla for making me listen.

I wished I had Frodo's ring so I could put it on and disappear. Not that Frodo ever had a stupid problem like this. All he had to deal with was mortal danger.

After Claire strolled off to the bathroom in search of her eye shadow, I told Kayla I wanted to go home and take a shower. I walked home even though Kayla's mom offered to drive me.

I scuffed along on the sandy edges of the streets. The sun was bright, and glittery bits of rock and sand scattered in front of my feet.

I hated Kayla. When I came across a baseball-size rock, I gave it a good kick.

Kayla was my first real friend after we moved here—Shipley, North Carolina—at the start of third grade. I missed the hills and trees of Asheville, where we lived before. Our house in Asheville was out in the country, with woods all around, and I'd loved wandering there. Deer came right into our backyard, and in the woods there were quartz crystals in some of the rocks, and chipmunks and squirrels, and strange things, too—creepy cicada shells clinging to tree bark, mysterious holes where maybe snakes lived, and big fungus things that were orange or white or brown.

No mysteries here. Everything flat as a board, and not so many trees. Shipley was a half hour from the coast—a flat, sandy, tiny little town. I did like the beaches, and chasing waves and finding shells. But right in Shipley there was nothing. I mean *zero*. Downtown was about three little stores in old brick buildings. There was one medium-size grocery store, and no place at all to shop for clothes or see a movie in a real theater, unless you counted the mall where Daddy worked, which was at least ten miles away, down the road toward New Bern. I don't think Shipley had any big companies for people to work in, except maybe the furniture factory and the chicken-processing plant.

In Asheville, everywhere you looked there were movie theaters and pizza places and malls and bowling alleys and ice-cream stores and parks—there was always something to do. I started calling our new town Sleepy Shipley, that August when we moved here, when I couldn't believe how small it was, and how the heat settled like a blanket over everything. There were hardly any sidewalks, and big grasshoppers whirred along the edges of the streets in the Bermuda grass and the hot, glinting sand.

I didn't call it Sleepy Shipley out loud except at home, after the time I said it in front of Kayla and she got mad. We were new friends then, early in the school year, and we were so crazy about hanging around together that I wasn't being careful about what I said. And of course Mama was right when she said, later, "Well, what do you expect? This is Kayla's home." Kayla was born in Shipley, and her father ran the furniture factory. Her mother sold houses and her name was on signs all over the place. The Mortons were pretty important in Shipley, I guess.

I had to apologize to Kayla then, and she forgave me and it was all right. But now I wanted to insult her again. *Sleepy Shipley*, I thought. *Kayla Moron Morton, queen of Sleepy Shipley*.

I tramped along past smooth flat lawns, palmettos, clumps of grasses as tall as me. A right turn, a long stretch down Bowman Street, then a left on Grady Street, and our house the fourth on the left. An average-size, red-brick house. Same flat lawn as all the other places around here, a palmetto at the corner of the lot, pink azaleas by the front door.

Ordinarily, walking by myself, I'd be Frodo tramping across fields and mountains, or maybe Arwen galloping toward Rivendell to save Frodo, or Aragorn tracking Merry and Pippin after the Uruk-hai captured them. But this time I didn't feel like it. The whole way home all those mad, ashamed feelings and all those thoughts about Kayla and Claire and Monica and me were like boxers slugging it out in my stomach and my head. I kept picturing my sister in her dumb jacket, and Claire smirking, and all those loud boys making fun of Monica.

Another thought was hanging around on the fringes, but I ignored it. Until this morning, when I woke up with it heavy in my head, as if it had sneaked up during the night.

How could I be *anybody* in middle school, with Monica for a sister?

Chapter 2

Thinking About Monica

Until now, I hadn't thought that much about Monica. She'd always just been there, like our parents. Sure, she was kind of weird—I'd known that for a while. She didn't get along with people very well, and she'd never had any real friends. Maybe that was why she didn't like school much, even though her grades weren't bad.

She liked sports, but she never joined any teams. She watched games on TV with Mama and Daddy, especially basketball and baseball. Sometimes she'd shoot baskets next door, where the Lovingers had a hoop at the end of their driveway; Mrs. Lovinger had told us we could use it anytime. At the pool, she swam by herself.

My bedroom and Monica's were side by side and just alike—identical beds and dressers and desks, and the same pale pink walls and pink flowered curtains. Both of us had always had our beds next to the wall that separated our rooms, and when we were little we'd lie in bed and knock on the wall, back and forth, pretending to have a secret code or beating out the rhythm of a song. Each of us would try to guess what song the other one was tapping, and we'd giggle and call back and forth until Mama or Daddy would say, "Hush up in there! Go to sleep."

Anyway, that was when we were little.

There was just one big difference between Monica's bedroom and mine: hers had a wide, shallow wooden box with a chicken-wire cover that took up the whole middle of the floor, leaving only a narrow path from the door to the closet to the desk to the bed. Inside the box were three guinea pigs. They were all the shaggy kind, the ones that look like a cross between a sheepdog and a rat.

The guinea pigs were kind of cute, I guess, but I was never crazy about them. Our dog, Bruce, was the only pet I needed—except a horse, which I knew I was never going to get. Bruce could chase sticks and tennis balls, and he didn't have to be kept in a cage in the house. When I came home from school he jumped all over me, he was so glad to see me. What good was a guinea pig compared to that?

But Monica adored her pigs. She took them out and played with them a lot, and she was always taking bits of vegetables from the kitchen to feed them. She even kept their box clean, most of the time. Sometimes she seemed to like playing with her guinea pigs better than playing with other kids.

Another thing about Monica was that she always thought she could boss me around. Like being two years older gave her the right to tell me what to do. Once, when I was in first grade, she tried to make me carry her backpack home from the school-bus stop, but I dropped it and just kept walking. She had to go back and get it.

She didn't try that again, but she was always telling me to clean my room, and if I was folding my clothes or making a paper airplane or peeling an orange, she'd say I was doing it wrong. "You don't know how to do it. *Kid*," she'd say.

Of course, lots of people think their brothers and sisters are weird. But I knew Monica was *really* strange. People were probably laughing at her all the time. Saying she was ugly and goofy. Avoiding sitting next to her at lunch. She was so weird, it was hysterically funny if she liked a cute boy.

I never thought Monica's strangeness had much to do with me. Until now.

When fall came we'd be in the same school. Everybody would realize right away that we were sisters—after all, we were the only Chaney family in town. Most of the seventh and eighth graders wouldn't know me at all, but they'd know my sister. They'd probably figure I had to be just like Monica.

What kind of a way to start middle school was that?

A few days after my visit to Kayla's house, I went downstairs as soon as I woke up, pausing at the window by the landing to see what kind of day it was. Sunny, and Sunday-morning quiet. I could hear a murmur from my dad and a rattle of newspaper. I couldn't see from the stairs, but I knew that he and Mama were sitting on the screened porch drinking coffee and reading the paper. They did that till church time every Sunday if the weather was good. They always moved slow in the morning, especially Sundays.

Some mornings I ran out and hugged them, and jumped up and down to make the cups and saucers rattle, till Daddy folded up a section of newspaper and pretended to swat me with it. But today I didn't feel like it. I passed by Monica, who was on the couch reading the comics, and went to the refrigerator for orange juice.

Then I put the juice on the coffee table and flopped into the big brown armchair. I stared across the table at Monica, who had her basket of yarn and knitting needles on the couch beside her. I didn't know anybody who knitted except old ladies and a few women my mother's age. And the way Monica dressed and acted was kind of tomboyish, so it was funny that she liked knitting.

As far as I could tell, she knew only one stitch. She never made anything except different-colored squares that she was planning to sew together to make a throw or a bedspread or something.

For now, though, she was concentrating on the comics. I concentrated on *her*, scalp to toenails, trying to see her the way I would if I'd never met her before. Trying to figure out if you could tell just by looking how weird she was.

Hair: short, wavy, medium brown, not very clean. Good haircut? Not really. Sort of old-ladyish.

My hair, by the way, was exactly the same color, but longer, almost to my shoulders, straight, with bangs.

Face: kind of wide. Not really ugly but definitely not pretty. Blue eyes, a few freckles, a chin that looked determined. No makeup, but after all it was first thing in the morning. Though Monica never wore makeup, had never even tried mascara or lip gloss.

I didn't think we looked the least bit alike, no matter what my aunt Brenda said about our matching eyes and hair. Brenda and a lot of other people said we looked Irish like our dad, even though we didn't have red hair like him.

Clothes: pajamas, basic cotton: boxy shirt with buttons, same as she'd always worn.

Same kind I wore.

I looked down at my own pj's, printed with kittens playing on clouds. Monica's, with bunches of flowers, were old and a little tight.

Body: taller than average, and as thin as Claire, but the opposite of willowy—awkward, with elbows and knees always sticking out. For at least a year she'd been wearing a bra and getting her period every month. She was secretive, like I was too young to know about it or something—really annoying. I hadn't gotten a period yet, even though most of the girls in my class probably had, and my breasts barely stuck out the tiniest bit.

I wasn't exactly jealous about that. I didn't know what I was.

Anyway, back to Monica.

Legs: ordinary—except hairy because she never shaved them, which I was pretty sure all the other seventh-grade girls did. Even a few of the fifth graders, including Kayla, shaved their legs, which Mama said was ridiculous.

Toes: propped on the edge of the coffee table. The usual number on each foot, all in their natural color. My own toes, I noticed suddenly, were lined up on the table, too, directly across from Monica's, like checkers at the start of a game. I examined the slightly chipped purple polish that Kayla and I had put on a week earlier, and though I didn't like the color that much, I felt kind of cool compared to Monica.

I didn't know what all this added up to. What I wondered now was, how come every time I tried to figure out some part of Monica, I ended up talking about me?

An hour later we walked into church, into the education building for Sunday school, right behind Claire and Kayla. This was the biggest of the three Baptist churches in Shipley, and the only one that both black and white people went to. We went practically every Sunday, always feeling a little stiff because we were wearing our best dresses. Mama said we had to, even though some kids just wore regular school clothes.

Mama was dressed up even more than usual for a Sunday, in a new spring dress that was two layers, plain lavender underneath and see-through fabric printed with lavender and white flowers on top. She had a white purse over her shoulder and her old white Bible in one hand. Even though she didn't look cool like the high-school and college girls, I thought she looked good, for a mom. Her hair was brown like mine and Monica's, only darker, except for some gray here and there.

Mama's so lucky—she always looks like she has a tan. Daddy says she must have had a Cherokee or a Choctaw back in her family somewhere, or maybe an Italian. Monica and I are pale, like Daddy, and every summer they're both after us to wear sunscreen.

"Straighten your belt, Erin," Mama said, and Daddy said, "So long, ladies," as they went on down the hall to the grownups' classes. Daddy was wearing the same kind of boring suit he wore to work every day, and his red hair was slicked down, and he shook hands with all the men, and said things like "How do, Sam," and "Mornin', Brother Mackesey."

At least today wasn't one of his Irish days, when he went around saying "Top of the mornin' to you" and "Sure, and begorra" and stuff like that. It was so embarrassing. He kind of looked Irish and he liked the idea of being Irish, and that's why Monica and I got these Irish names. Every now and then in church during silent prayer, I remembered to thank the Lord that I'd gotten a normal Irish name instead of a weird one like Monica.

Mama said he was about as Irish as any other hillbilly from Buncombe County, North Carolina.

Monica and I went to the big Youth Room, which had all kinds of games and books, and big soft couches, and small rooms for classes off to the side. Ahead of us, Claire sailed over to three or four other seventh-grade girls. They were talking and laughing and swinging their purses and fiddling with necklaces.

Claire slipped into their group, and they all bobbed around in a loose circle, like goldfish in a plastic bag. Instead of going past them, toward Kayla and some other kids I knew, I hung back, watching. I already knew Monica wasn't friends with these girls—not one of them had ever been to our house. In fact, Monica never had friends come over. But I wanted to see what she'd say to them and how they'd answer. I wanted to see what middle school might be like.

In a few minutes we'd all have to go to our classes, but for now everybody was in the big room, talking and laughing. A second grader was showing off her ballet steps, and a couple of boys my age were shoving each other in a stiff-armed way that was supposed to be funny.

Monica didn't hesitate. She marched right over to Claire's little group, to an opening in the loose circle. "Hi," she said, to nobody in particular. The conversation, about the new swimming pool that was being built at Melissa's house, didn't even pause.

"Mama says I can have a pool party as soon as it's done," Melissa was saying.

"I have to get a new bathing suit before I get in a pool this year," said Cindy. "My old one is so awful."

"They have really cute ones at Barton's," said Madeline. Barton's was a big, fancy department store in the huge mall in Raleigh. Too expensive for us, Mama said. We always shopped at the local Stockdale's, a much smaller department store, because Daddy was the manager and we got a discount. Stockdale's was okay, but it wasn't glamorous like Barton's, where pretty women were always coming up to you with samples of perfumes and makeup.

"I love Barton's," Cindy sighed.

"Well, I love Stockdale's," Monica put in abruptly. Like a loyal bulldog. Almost as if Cindy's loving Barton's was some kind of personal insult. All the girls knew perfectly well that our father worked at Stockdale's.

Claire tittered, then Melissa too, and Madeline and Cindy looked down, trying to stifle giggles, darting sideways smirks at each other.

I felt hot all over. Suddenly I wondered how I looked, standing by myself and eavesdropping. I pretended to be searching for something in my purse.

Nobody answered Monica; they went on talking about bathing suits and pools. Monica just stood there in her stiff, square-shouldered way, but she must have realized they were laughing at her, because her face was red and she wasn't saying a word.

I didn't have to keep standing there listening. I could go find a friend to talk to—far away from Monica. But I was determined to get the whole picture of how she fit—or didn't fit—into the seventh grade. Which—after another month of school and then a summer—would be the eighth grade, and me in sixth, seeing them every day in middle school.

Melissa was saying, "Should I invite Tim and Josh?" They were brothers who had just moved here, and they were really cute. I'd heard about them from Kayla, who got it from Claire, of course.

The girls giggled. "Mm-*hmm*," said Claire.

Suddenly Monica said, "Can I come?"

There was just a second's pause before Melissa said, very sweetly and very fast, "Oh, everybody's coming, but it won't be for ages. You know, they've barely started digging the hole, and after it's all done, my parents want to have a grown-ups' party. So after that. Maybe."

No way would Monica get invited to that party, I thought, and she probably didn't even know it.

At that moment Cindy tugged urgently on Madeline's arm, pulling her away from the group. They hurried past me, arm in arm, almost doubled over laughing, and Cindy gasped, "*Monica* wants to come to the pool party!" The two of them went out to the hall, laughing harder than ever.

Suddenly I couldn't stand to watch any more of this. I turned away, looking for a group to take me in. Now, though, it seemed like everybody but me was part of a tight little group. Closed.

I wasn't about to go up to a bunch of boys, or the little first or second or third graders. I wished Hannah was there, but she was a Catholic. Jane-Marie and Samantha were over in a corner, and I talked to them pretty often at school and sometimes sat with them at lunch. But they were very cool kids, and best friends with each other, and right now they looked like they were having a serious talk. Maybe they wouldn't want me to come up to them.

Shakara was there, hugging her little kindergarten brother, Clifton, whose dark, tear-tracked face rested against the lighter brown of her arm. I went over to them. "Hi, Shakara. What's wrong with Clifton?"

"He doesn't feel good," Shakara said. "I better take him to find Mama. Come on, Clif, let's go find Mama." They turned toward the door, and my one minute of feeling comfortable with someone was over. I looked around again, wondering who I could talk to so I wouldn't look like a person with no friends.

Kayla! I was relieved to spot her, standing by a window with Danielle. I knew Danielle was her best friend now—it hadn't been me for a long time—but I was used to that, and really it was okay. Kayla and I were still friends; we knew each other really well. At her house the other day she hadn't been so nice, but maybe that was my fault for being so cranky about soccer.

I walked right over to them. "Hey, Kayla. Hi, Danielle." They both said hi.

"What's going on?" I said brightly, though I didn't feel bright. But before I even finished the words, Kayla tossed her shimmery hair, murmured something to Danielle, and slowly, but very definitely, turned her back on me. I stared at the back of her head and the hair fanned out over her shoulders. I glimpsed surprise on Danielle's face.

My cheeks were suddenly hot. For a moment I couldn't move, and then I jerked my gaze away from Danielle's startled eyes and walked off, moving quickly out into the hall and toward the water fountain.

All I did was say hi and "What's going on?" Was there something wrong with how I said it? Was I butting in? "Butt in" was what Monica did. She could stand in a group all day and never be part of the conversation, just now and then blurt out some dumb thing. Had Kayla decided she didn't want to be friends with someone who had a dorky sister like Monica? Or had she just decided she didn't like *me*?

I lingered around the water fountain, bending down to get a drink whenever someone walked by so that I wouldn't have to talk to anyone.

Idiot, I said to myself, watching the water swirl down the bright, stainless-steel drain. *All this time you've been worrying about how people in middle school might figure you're just like Monica. Never mind that—what if you really* are *just like Monica?*

Chapter 3

Playground

"*Shew! Shew! Shew!*" Ricky Talmadge, playing Legolas, shot arrow after arrow from an imaginary bow, aiming into a group of kids lining up for kickball.

Next to Ricky were Sam Lyons and Jesse Miller, but they weren't watching him; they were head-to-head. "*I'm* Aragorn," said Sam, folding his arms. "I said it first."

"You were Aragorn last time. You always have to be Aragorn," Jesse said in an accusing tone. "That is so unfair."

"You gotta be Gimli. I said Aragorn first, and somebody's gotta be Gimli."

"I'm not being a dumb dwarf."

Ricky turned and shot at Luke Sullivan, a big hulk of a

boy who never minded being a bad guy and was thrusting out his chin and baring his teeth and growling like an Uruk-hai. He clutched his chest and collapsed slowly onto the ground, twitching.

"Look, we're wasting our recess," said Sam. "How about you be an Uruk-hai, and we just won't have a Gimli."

Jesse was scowling and kicking at the wood chips, but finally said okay.

I was swinging right beside them, watching. "Hey," I said to Sam. "Isn't anybody going to be Frodo? I could be him."

"Don't need Frodo. We're fighting, can't you tell?" he answered.

"Fight, fight, fight," I mocked, but he had already run off, hacking at Jesse and Luke with his imaginary sword. The boys played *The Lord of the Rings* all the time, but the only part they liked was the fighting.

I pumped the swing, higher and higher, thinking what dummies boys were, and how they didn't have a clue about all the beautiful, noble themes in *The Lord of the Rings*. How the brave little hobbits go into terrible danger even though they aren't fighters. How the immortal Arwen loves the mortal Aragorn, knowing that he will age and die. How friends are absolutely loyal and will face any peril to help each other.

Anyway, I could sword-fight as well as any boy, if I *was* part of their dumb game.

I missed playing pretend games like that. Most of the

fifth-grade girls had quit doing that kind of thing. Or, if they did play a pretend game, they only wanted girls' parts. So then who could you be in *The Lord of the Rings*? Galadriel was kind of cool, I thought. She was powerful and beautiful, and so was Arwen, in a different way. But they weren't that important, and they didn't have a lot of adventures.

I pulled back on the chains, pumping, and hung my head back. Chunks of blue-and-white sky, cut by the poles of the swing set, swayed dizzily above me. I wanted to be something great, right now. I wanted to be as beautiful as Arwen and bold as Aragorn and noble as Frodo. I wanted some wild, on-my-own adventure in foreign lands.

At the peak of the upswing I flung myself out over a vast precipice in the mines of Moria. "Yaaah!" I landed with a thump but couldn't keep my footing and fell onto my butt. I got up and brushed off the wood chips, a little daunted by my awkward landing but still feeling the rush of flight.

A silvery laugh made me look up. Kayla and Danielle and Jane-Marie were nearby, leaning on the climbing structure and watching me. The laugh was Kayla's.

"Erin," she said, all sweet and smiley, as if she was talking to a kindergartner, "are you playing Tarzan?" The other two giggled and grinned, and Danielle said, "Tarzan, queen of the jungle!" You could always count on stupid Danielle to copy anything Kayla did. Lately she'd started swinging her blond hair around like Kayla, even though Danielle's wasn't nearly so long and golden. In fact, it was kind of stringy and the color was dirty blond.

My face was hot, and I swiped at the wood chips still clinging to my shorts. I leaned over and pulled more wood chips from between my feet and my thick sandals.

All three of them were wearing skirts and delicate, girlie sandals. Kayla was even wearing stockings. All three wore their hair in ponytails held by scrunchies that matched their outfits. It was like they were almost grown up and I was a grubby little kid.

"I'm not playing Tarzan, I'm just swinging," I said without looking straight at any of them. Then I walked away from their smirking faces toward the school, feeling them watching. I was awkward and hot and ugly and stupid.

I was like Monica.

Out of their sight, I sat down on the low wall that separated the climbing structures from the paved part where kids were playing kickball. I watched the game for a while, occasionally glancing back uneasily, but I didn't see Kayla and her crew anywhere.

Finally, with only five minutes of recess left, Hannah came out of the building. Mrs. Winsted had made her stay in to finish the math worksheet. "Math, Hannah," Mrs. Winsted had said. "Not doodling. Not whispering."

Hannah ran straight to the monkey bars, crossed them hand over hand, and dropped down. Then she came over and sat next to me, tucking her smooth brown hair behind her ears.

Hannah had a small nose and mouth, and her grin was a little bit crooked. She wasn't as pretty as some of the other girls, but she had the most wide-awake face I'd ever seen. Whenever you were around Hannah you felt that something exciting could happen. You looked at that grin and thought that whatever came next just might be fun.

Or, if you were a teacher, you thought it just might be trouble. Not really bad trouble, though—more like mischief. Mrs. Winsted, for instance, seemed to like Hannah, but you could tell she was keeping a close eye on her.

I told Hannah what had happened, leaving out the way I yelled "yaaah" as I flew out of the swing.

"You know what Kayla is?" Hannah said thoughtfully, gazing over at the kickball game. "*Prissy*. I can't stand prissy girls."

I clenched my hands on the gritty edge of the wall we were sitting on. "I'm gonna get her back."

"How?"

I didn't have an answer to that.

Yet.

Chapter 4

The McLarens

"I'm the one who ought to be spoiled," Hannah said one day in her living room after school. "I'm the youngest—I should be the princess around here." She paced restlessly around the room, then scooped up the family's long-haired white cat, who was dozing on the windowsill and looked wide-eyed and startled for a moment before settling into Hannah's arms. "Like you, you beautiful baby, you sweet sweet kitty."

Hannah had two sisters—both of them pretty—and one brother, who was everybody's pet, Hannah always said, because he was the only boy. Catherine, the oldest, was in college, somewhere way off. Then came Laura—Miss Perfect,

Hannah called her—who was in high school and was really smart and played the cello. Those things might have made her seem a little weird, except that she also had delicate features and curly brown hair, and she was fun to be around. She really was just about perfect, as far as I could see, even though I knew exactly how Hannah would snort if I said so.

The third McLaren was Jake—eighth grader, nonstop joker, and probably the most popular boy in his grade. Last of all was Hannah.

She dropped the cat, a little abruptly, and it strolled out of the room. Jake, she complained, never had to do any housework, just because he was a boy. Everybody made a fuss over Catherine when she was home from college. Laura was Miss Perfect, with her fabulous grades and her talent for music. All their clothes got handed down to Hannah.

I'd heard most of this before, but usually Hannah was funny when she talked about it. Today there was a bitter edge to her voice, as though everything was getting to her.

"Catherine and Laura are such pain-in-the-butt *good examples*," Hannah said. "You're lucky to have only one sister."

Lucky? I looked at the framed picture of the four kids and their parents that sat on the end table by the couch. It had been taken last summer, when they went hiking in Maine, and they were all sitting on a big rock in the sun, and the wind was blowing their hair back, and they were all good-looking and happy and confident.

Mr. McLaren sat on one end of the rock, with his arm

around Hannah. He had a big, cheerful grin, and the sun gleamed off the bald circle on top of his head. Mrs. McLaren sat between Hannah and Jake, with Laura and Catherine in back, leaning on their mother's shoulders.

Our family pictures always looked awkward somehow—somebody's eyes were closed, or somebody's collar was twisted. This looked like a photo from an L.L. Bean catalog. Catherine, Laura, Jake, and Hannah looked like the kind of kids who couldn't possibly have any idea what it felt like to be ashamed of your sister, or yourself.

All this flashed through my mind, and then I saw Hannah watching me with a strange expression on her face.

"What?" I said.

"The perfect family, right?" she burst out sarcastically. "There we are, the happy McLarens."

She turned quickly away, as though she didn't want me to see her face, and took a few aimless steps before flopping down on the far end of the couch, still with her face averted.

For a few seconds I was too stunned to say anything. In the silence I could hear Jake talking on the phone in the kitchen and Laura practicing some mournful piece on her cello upstairs.

"Hannah?" I said at last, uncertainly. "What—what's wrong?"

At first she didn't answer, and I sat down on the couch, a couple of feet from her, and waited. She picked up a Rubik's Cube from the table beside her and turned it in her hands, not moving the pieces, just staring at the unsolved jumble of colored squares on every side.

"My dad's moving out," she said flatly.

"Oh no," I breathed.

"Oh yes. He said so last night. He's said it before, but this time he's really packing. He's got an apartment, and he's going to take his things over there this weekend."

It made sense, and it didn't make any sense at all. Now I remembered times when Hannah had mentioned her parents having terrible fights; now I remembered overhearing Mrs. McLaren complain to Mama that her husband traveled so much for his job, he hardly knew his own kids.

On the other hand, Mr. McLaren was always so *nice*. I didn't see him often, but whenever I did, he told me how tall and pretty I was getting, and he asked about my family and even Bruce, our dog. He made me feel like he was really interested in the answers.

And Mrs. McLaren was nice, too. She was kind of fat but very brisk and neat, and she was always helping with things at school, like special science projects. I didn't see why they couldn't get along.

Hannah was twisting the pieces of the Rubik's Cube now. One side, I could see, was completely orange, and she was trying to make another one all green, but bits of red and yellow kept interfering, and every time she tried to fix the green side, the orange one got messed up.

"I'm really sorry, Hannah," I said. "That's so sad."

"Yeah," she said, staring at the cube.

Later I biked home, and as soon as I got to our driveway, Bruce raced around from the backyard to jump all over me. Bruce thought everybody in the entire world was his friend, but especially our family. You couldn't really say what kind of dog he was—just a medium-size dog with a smooth brown coat. Maybe there was some beagle in him, Mama said, but basically he was a Heinz 57. Daddy said that whatever he was, he was no watchdog.

I got off my bike and rubbed his head and his belly, and played with his floppy ears. We'd gotten him from the animal shelter in Asheville, and when we first moved to Shipley and I didn't have any friends, he could always make me feel better. I'd come home from this strange new school and let him lick my face, and I'd think that somehow things were going to be okay.

If my dad was moving out, would Bruce make me feel any better? What would it feel like, to have your father leaving? Just trying to imagine it was making a hole inside me, even as Bruce was licking my ear.

Not that Mama and Daddy would ever split up. They didn't fight—well, not much. Then I remembered a Saturday a few weeks earlier, when I'd walked into the house to hear angry voices upstairs. I couldn't catch any of the words—they must have heard the door opening, because the voices dropped immediately.

I'd gone into the dining room and was looking through

the mail that lay on the table when Mama came hurrying downstairs. She didn't even pause, just said, "Hello, Erin," in a grim voice and kept walking fast to the back door. It slammed behind her, and a minute later, looking out the window, I saw her with a hoe in her hand, heading for the garden.

Two minutes after that Daddy came downstairs, snapped at me for leaving my room a mess, and launched into a lecture about how kids today have too much stuff and don't appreciate any of it and never take care of anything and don't know how to work hard and never save a dime and on and on and on.

He made me go upstairs to clean my room, and I went without a word, gritting my teeth, my heart pounding with resentment. While I was hanging up clothes I heard him go out the front door, get in the car, and drive away. A little later I went out to the garden and asked Mama what she and Daddy were fighting about. "Grown-up things," she answered shortly, and yanked out a blighted tomato plant.

Now Bruce followed me into the carport, where I put my bike away. I looked down at his eager face, and thought, *You mutt. You're sweet, but you don't know* anything *about human beings.*

I gave him one last hug and went inside.

Monica was doing her homework on the dining-room table, with her books and papers spread out all over. She was scrubbing industriously at a sheet of notebook paper with a big pink eraser. "Where've you been?" she said as I walked by her toward the kitchen.

"Hannah's," I answered.

"Did Mama say you could go over there?"

"None of your beeswax." I could see Mama out the window, planting something in her vegetable garden. She loved digging in the dirt. This probably meant that dinner would be late, and I was already hungry.

"It's my beeswax if I say it is."

I ignored this and stood by the window a minute longer, watching Mama. What Hannah had told me, and thinking about Mama and Daddy fighting, had left me enveloped in a heavy cloud of worry. Parents were so mysterious—who could figure out the things they did?

I glanced over at Monica, who had gone back to her homework, and suddenly a rush of anguish overwhelmed me. I *needed* a sister. I needed a sister I could talk to, who would understand these worries about parents and reassure me. I needed a sister who would break ground for me—start dating, try out hairstyles, bend a few rules. I needed a sister who could teach me about music and boys and makeup and middle school—a sister to look up to and be proud of.

Monica was *nothing* like that ideal sister, and never would be.

I went into the kitchen and rummaged around, but everything looked unappealing. Finally I ate a handful of stale crackers.

When I walked through the dining room again, Monica was staring at me, for some reason. Just the sight of her staring suddenly irritated me so much, I couldn't stand it.

I stopped, leaned forward, shaping my hands into binoculars, and stared back. "Duh, like it's a person, like I've never seen a person before," I said in a dumb voice.

She turned red and said, "Oh shut up."

This was a weak response and so, more or less satisfied, I started toward my room. But Monica had thought of something else to say. "Bet you haven't done your homework."

"Big deal, I'll get it done."

"You have to get it done before dinner."

"No I don't."

"Oh yes you do." Very superior tone.

"Look," I said. "When I go to a friend's house after school, I do homework later, okay?"

"You just think the rules don't apply to you."

"You know what, Monica?" I said this slowly, deliberately. "You could do it this way too, if you had any friends. But you don't."

Her face was redder than ever now. I caught one brief glimpse of it and went straight to my room so I wouldn't have to look at her.

I felt mean and guilty. But I told myself it was Monica's fault, for being so bossy.

Chapter 5

Volcano Day

School was almost over, only three weeks to go. Every morning Kayla gave me a big "Hi, Erin!" with a big fakey smile. But that was all she ever said to me, and I stayed away from her. I'd hardly be able to talk to her even if I wanted to, since she and Danielle were practically glued together.

I looked at them sometimes, whispering in class or walking down the hall together, Kayla's shimmery gold hair swaying and Danielle's slightly darker, slightly shorter hair swaying the same way, and I wished I had a best friend like that. I did have friends, of course—I wasn't like Monica. At recess I either played kickball with a bunch of kids, mostly boys, or else I played with Hannah, or Samantha and Jane-

Marie, or Shakara or Rachel. Sometimes I did something with them after school.

The one I liked best was Hannah, but we weren't best friends. Hannah didn't have a best friend. She'd always been friendly with all kinds of people, even the ones that nobody liked. But lately she was hanging out more with me. She told me I was the first person she'd told about her dad moving out. She told me how it had taken him three trips in his car to get all his stuff to his new apartment that Saturday, and how Mrs. McLaren had gone on an all-day shopping trip with one of her friends so she wouldn't have to watch, and Laura had stayed in her room and wouldn't say a word to him, not even good-bye.

Jake had played football in the backyard with three of his friends for hours, as if he didn't even notice what was going on, but when their dad came to the backyard before the last trip to say good-bye, Jake started crying and his friends went home.

"What did you do?" I asked Hannah.

"Well, I didn't cry," she said proudly. "I told him he was a jerk. I put sand in the suitcase with all his pajamas and underwear." But there were glimmers of tears in her eyes when she said it.

The fifth-grade classroom was buzzing all the time. We'd had the tour of Marsh Middle School, and ever since we hadn't felt like fifth graders anymore. We'd seen Marsh's huge gym, the auditorium, the long halls lined with lockers, each with its own secret combination lock. We'd seen the kids, some of them not much bigger than us, who swarmed through the halls between classes and packed the cafeteria at lunchtime and dressed like teenagers. We'd seen all that, and we were done with elementary school.

Back at Sandy Creek we were restless, ready for something to happen. And things *were* happening—all the end-of-the-year events that always made the last few weeks of school a blur, only this year everything was final. It was the last time we'd go to the K-2 choral concert, the last time we'd watch the third and fourth graders put on a play. And, one bright, hot afternoon, it was our last Volcano Day.

On Volcano Day anybody who wanted to could go out on the playground, an hour before school ended, and set off their own homemade baking-soda-and-vinegar volcano. This year, Hannah made the biggest volcano anyone had ever seen. Her mother had to help carry it into school that morning. It was in a wide, shallow cardboard box, and it was over two feet high and made of plaster of paris, and it must have had about five pounds of baking soda in it. She brought a quart bottle of white vinegar to set it off.

Some of us sent our own pathetic little lava flows fizzing down miniature slopes, then gathered around to see what Hannah's would do. Even Mrs. Winsted came over to watch.

Hannah looked all around, holding the bottle of vinegar, waiting while her audience grew. She was loving the attention—I could see that in her face, in the excitement that danced in her eyes—but she looked determined, too, almost as if she thought someone might try to stop her.

"Come on, Hannah Banana," Ricky said impatiently. "Let's see it."

She pretended not to hear him, but a few seconds later she knelt in front of the volcano. She'd painted it black, with streaks of red and orange flowing from the crater and down the sides. But she didn't pour the vinegar yet. She reached into her pocket and pulled out something small, then set it carefully on the lip of the crater.

She sat back on her heels, looking it over, while everyone else stared and laughed. It was a LEGO man, sitting there with his tiny legs jutting out over the volcano's mouth.

"He's gonna get sizzled." Ricky, who was standing next to me, grinned.

"Fry him!" Jesse hooted.

"Give him a surfboard," somebody else yelled.

All the laughing and talking died down as Hannah took the top off the vinegar bottle and raised it over the volcano. In the relative quiet, Mrs. Winsted said, "Who is that, Hannah?"

And just before she poured, and the baking soda and vinegar bubbled madly out the top and down the sides, tumbling the LEGO man down the slope into the cardboard wasteland at the bottom, Hannah answered, "My father."

Chapter 6
___

Balcony Scene

By the last week of school I was excited and Monica was grumpy. All week I kept thinking, *I'm out of here!* Mrs. Winsted kept telling us, "School is not over, kids. We still have work to do." But there was a lot of giggling and fooling around, and even Mrs. Winsted didn't seem all that serious about the work.

With everybody giddy like this, it wasn't too hard to forget my worries about Monica and Kayla and Hannah. And myself.

Every morning on the way to school I was as brave as Aragorn, ready to fling myself into battle, slashing the air with a stick sword. Or I was Legolas the tall elf, swift and light, more nimble than any human, leaping into the saddle as if I was flying.

Monica, though, was anything but winged. She dragged her feet in the morning, getting ready for school as if she was going to the doctor for a shot. After school she spent more time than ever with the guinea pigs, and she was even bossier than usual, asking me if I'd done my homework or telling me to get my stuff off the table.

On Wednesday, when we were supposed to help Mama fix dinner, instead of waiting for Mama to tell us what to do, she ordered me around. "I'll make the salad. Erin, you set the table."

"Nay nay, horseface." I was feeling too cheerful to be seriously annoyed; besides, I was pleased to have come up with this clever answer, which I'd heard on the playground the week before. I continued reading the advice column in the newspaper, where a woman wanted to know what to do about her teenage son who smoked marijuana.

"Erin," said Mama in her warning voice.

"Yes, Mama dearest?" I answered pleasantly.

"Be polite to your sister, and set the table."

"Coming, dearest Mama."

I finished the advice column, then went to the kitchen and started counting out forks and knives from the drawer. Instant rhythm: pick up one fork and one knife simultaneously, clink them together ("One!"), put them on the counter, do it again. Pick up, *clink*, "Two!" *Clatter*. Pick up, *clink*, "Three!"

"Cut it out, dummy," snapped Monica.

"Girls," said Mama. "Would you please stop antagonizing each other?"

"Just making a little music," I said with a shrug, and took the silverware into the dining room.

Behind me, I heard Mama say, "Monica, what's going on, honey? Did you have a bad day at school?"

"No."

"Are you sure? You're acting kind of mad at the world."

"I'm not mad at the world." But she sure sounded like it.

Mama sighed. "If you say so." She took a casserole dish out of the oven and lifted the lid. A little cloud of steam puffed out.

"Good evening, ladies," called Daddy from the front hall.

Five minutes later we were all sitting in the dining room, and Daddy said, exactly the way he said almost every night at supper, "Well, how was everybody's day today?"

"Twenty-nine SUVs! Fourteen vans! And the highlight of the day—one white stretch limousine!" Mama worked part-time as a teller at a drive-in bank. Her job was so boring, she kept count of the different kinds of cars that came through.

"Very good," said Daddy. "And how was Sandy Creek School?"

"Good," I answered. "We finished making the video about our science projects. Tomorrow we get to watch the whole thing."

"Do parents get to see this?" Mama asked, reaching over to put a spoonful of spinach on each of our plates.

"I think we're all going to get copies of it. You know what's really great?"

"What?" said Daddy, cutting into a pork chop.

"Only two more days of school and I'll never have to go back there again."

"That's fine," Daddy said. "And how about Miss Monica? How was your day today?"

Monica rolled her eyes. "How come you have to ask that every single day?"

Daddy looked annoyed, like underneath his usual polite self there was someone touchy and tired and not so polite. "It's a civil question, Monica. Civilized people ask each other how their day went. Now, how about a civil answer?"

Monica clamped her mouth shut in that bulldog way we all knew, but Mama intervened, saying smoothly, "Your English class had a video project, too, didn't you, Monica?"

"Yeah."

"And you had a part in it, didn't you?"

"Everybody had a part," Monica mumbled.

"What was your part?" Daddy asked, and got a mumbled reply that none of us seemed to catch.

I suddenly had an idea that made everything funny. Daddy said, "What?" and at the same time I said, "I know! Her part was Mumbling Monica! Monica the Merry Mumbler!" No one else seemed to think this was funny.

"How did it go?" asked Mama.

"It was dumb," she said, looking down at her napkin and twisting it. "We were all supposed to read these speeches from *Romeo and Juliet* and then play them back. So we could see how we sounded and whether we looked at the audience and things like that."

"Well, that doesn't sound too bad," Mama said, "if everybody had to do the same thing."

Monica just sat there, eyes on her plate, blinking a little. Blinking back tears, I suddenly realized.

"Did something else happen, honey?" Mama asked gently.

"Just"—she swallowed hard before going on—"a bunch of dumb boys started calling people names."

"Calling who names—you?" asked Mama.

"Yeah." I could hardly hear her now.

"Like what?"

"Oh, I don't know," Monica said, looking away, blinking rapidly.

Mama shook her head. "Just ignore them. Boys think they have to show off, doing things like that."

But I wanted to know what they said. "What did they call you?" No answer. Monica wasn't looking at any of us, just fiddling with her napkin, her glass of milk, her fork. "Come on, what did they call you?"

Mama and Daddy were waiting for an answer, too.

"Dumb stuff," she muttered finally. "Like 'Juliet.' When

we were going upstairs." Her voice got louder and angrier, doing a mocking imitation. "'There's Juliet on her balcony.'"

"What's wrong with that?" said Daddy. "That Juliet was a real pretty girl, if I remember rightly."

I rolled my eyes. Daddy just did not get it.

Monica didn't seem to hear him. "Then stupid Mark Malone said, 'Where's Romeo? Wherefore art thou Romeo?'" She was really beginning to cry now. "Stupid idiot."

"Of course he's an idiot," said Mama. "Pay no attention."

"And then," Monica said, and now she was swallowing hard and crying more. "And then he grabbed Randy Wayman"—a scrawny little guy—"and made him kneel down and lift his arms up. And then Randy pretended he had to throw up and all the boys started—barfing."

"Oh, that's nothing," Daddy said. "Don't let that bother you." He went on eating, but Mama winced, and I knew she didn't think it was "nothing." I suddenly didn't feel like eating anymore. I could hear the hoots of laughter, picture Monica's humiliated face.

Daddy went right on. Maybe he wanted to cheer her up by changing the subject. Or maybe, like I said, he just didn't get it. "Well, don't pay any attention to that sort of nonsense. Let me tell you about my day. Old Dad gets a turn, too, right?" He started talking about the people he interviewed for a salesclerk job in the shoe department, and how most of them didn't know the first thing about how to dress or how to act. Whenever you got good help, he said, they stayed a month or two, or a couple years at most, and then they left and you had to find somebody else.

I wasn't listening. I was thinking about how mean those kids were to my sister, and I wanted to kick that Mark Malone. I was thinking about how awful Monica must have felt, with all of them laughing at her. But I was also thinking, grimly, *Thanks a lot, Monica. Now I know who I'll be in middle school— Juliet's little sister.*

Chapter 7

The End of Fifth Grade

That evening Monica and I watched TV for a while, and she knitted while she watched. The show was about a big family, and the two sisters in it were always fighting and teasing each other. It was usually a funny show, but tonight it just irritated me—the things the girls fought about were so silly. In the middle of the show I got up and went to my room.

It was almost dark out, and the bit of sky that showed through my window, above the Lovingers' house next door, was deep deep blue. The Lovingers had two boys, both in high school, and I could see into one of their bedrooms, lit up, on the second floor. No one was in sight, just the upper shelves of a bookcase, with books and big gold sports trophies and a model battleship. I flipped on my light and the scene vanished.

My own room was kind of a mess. I looked around at the books and clothes and toys scattered on the floor and on the rumpled bed. There was a layer of dust on the framed pictures on top of my bookcase: a family trip to the beach, my cousin graduating from high school, Monica and me on her first day of kindergarten, Monica smiling behind me as I blew out six birthday candles.

There was one picture that my parents used on a Christmas card, and all my relatives said it was the cutest thing they'd ever seen. One of my grandmothers had taken it, and she had three copies made and framed them—a big one for my parents and small ones for Monica and me.

We were probably seven and five years old, and we were sitting on the front steps of our house in Asheville. Monica was reading to me from a book on her lap, and I was looking up at her adoringly. It was a bright day, and red tulips poked their heads up at the side of the steps, and both of us looked sweet and pretty. You could see why parents and grandparents would love this picture.

But whenever I glanced at it, the look on my face always amazed me. Had I ever adored my sister, the way I seemed to in this photo?

Monica *had* read to me, not just on the day of that picture, but lots of other days, too. She had tied my shoes and brushed my hair. We'd shared a dollhouse, and spent hours arranging furniture and making up stories about our dolls. We'd played in the sandbox, under the sprinkler, in a tent we made of a blanket and chairs. She was always bossy, and we fought sometimes, but we had fun too.

Somehow, both of us had changed.

I didn't touch the pictures, but I started cleaning up everything else. Books went on the bookcase, clothes in the dresser or the closet or the hamper in the bathroom. Earrings and bracelets in the jewelry box. I opened a drawer and pulled out the pictures I'd drawn with Kayla so long ago, and shoved them into the trash can.

All kinds of toys were still lying around—Barbies and other dolls, stuffed animals, Pokémon figures, marbles, a kit for making bead necklaces. I hesitated, feeling too old for most of this stuff but not quite knowing what to do with it. Finally I just started throwing it onto the closet floor, and was a little surprised to discover it felt good to throw something. First a couple of rag dolls thumped softly, then a puzzle in its cardboard box. Then I flung in Pokémon stuff, a half-open bag of marbles, a little purse full of key chains. There were shoes on the closet floor and things were landing in them—cat's-eye marbles, Squirtle and Charmander—but I didn't care.

Barbies went flying, with their stiff smiles and shiny dresses, *whack* against the back wall of the closet. Their perfect legs *whack*. Their perfect hair *whack*. Ken landed with a manly thud. Barbie shoes with pointy heels, Barbie hairbrushes and bikinis rained down on him.

Next I took my two favorite stuffed animals—Kitty, my old yellow cat, and Ricky Raccoon—and put them next to my pillow. The rest of them I piled on the highest shelf of the bookcase, right on top of the dusty pictures. The monkey fell to the floor, but I fastened his Velcro hands together and hung him over one of the top corners of the bookcase. He didn't look much like a wild creature swinging through jungle treetops—more like a prisoner hanging from a dungeon wall.

The next day, as soon as I got to my desk, I saw that Kayla had her eye on me. The first bell had just rung, and I was taking homework out of my backpack. Kayla was standing next to her own desk a few feet away, with one hand on her hip, her head a little to one side and that sheet of golden hair falling sideways, too. She was giving me a smug look that I didn't like at all. For sure, she knew all about Monica being Juliet and all the boys barfing.

I fussed with my books and papers and pencils, hoping she'd stay away. But just as I crouched down to squeeze my backpack under my desk, I saw her pink toenails, her thin-strapped sandals, right beside me.

I gave the backpack a shove and stood up. It wasn't just Kayla—she had Danielle and Jane-Marie with her. It was like she led them around on a string.

"Hey, Erin," she said.

"Hey."

She gave the other two a look, like they were in some secret club, then smirked at me. "I heard Monica was Juliet in the play."

I shrugged. "It wasn't a play. They just read some of the parts." The way Danielle and Jane-Marie were grinning, I could tell they'd already heard the story.

"Well, *anyway*"—she slipped a brush out of this little purse she carried and started brushing her hair—"somebody made Randy Wayman kneel down to Monica like he's Romeo and she's Juliet. And then he started throwing up—but not really—you know. Didn't you hear about it, Erin?"

"No, I—no. That's—that's really weird."

Kayla rolled her eyes. "Lord, how could you not hear about it? Everybody's heard about it."

"I don't know," I muttered. The second bell rang, but they didn't move toward their seats.

"Your sister is funny," Jane-Marie said.

"Funny in the head," giggled Danielle.

"Just a teensy bit *weird*," said Kayla.

"Whatever." I tried to say it like I totally didn't care. But the one word was drowned out by Mrs. Winsted saying, "In your seats, girls. Now."

Finally Friday came, the crazy last day of school, and that night in the gym we had the fifth-grade moving-up ceremony. Mr. Stimson, the principal, made a boring speech and gave each of us a book and a certificate. Then we sang a couple of songs that the music teacher had been making us practice forever. "A ring is round and has no end, that's how long I'm going to be your friend." And then this "Farewell Song," like we'd never see each other again, when in fact every one of us would be in the sixth grade together next fall at J. B. Marsh Middle School.

Through the whole ceremony, I felt like I was looking at this ugly old gym, and all of Sandy Creek Elementary, with new eyes, as if I was looking for the first time instead of the last.

The next day I woke and saw the whole summer out in front of me, a big slow drowsy thing, as if I'd stepped onto an enormous air mattress bobbing on the enormous ocean. This was a good comparison, I decided, since an enormous air mattress would be nearly impossible to steer, and I didn't get to steer my own summer very much, even though I was eleven years four months old and a graduate of Sandy Creek Elementary.

I wanted to go to Camp Mountain Glen, where Samantha and Jane-Marie had gone the summer before. Two weeks, or four or even six weeks, completely away from home, with horses to ride and canoeing and jewelry making and all kinds of cool things to do. Samantha stayed just two weeks, but Jane-Marie went for four, and this summer they were both going back for four weeks. I was dying to ride horses, which I'd only done a couple of times in my whole life. Plus it would be so great to be away from Monica for a month.

Mama looked doubtful the minute I mentioned it. "That's a long time away from home for a girl your age." She was putting dishes in the dishwasher and paused with two coffee mugs in her hands. "But you know, maybe if Monica went, too . . ." She trailed off, considering, then peered hard into my face. "Well?"

I must have looked horrified, because I was. Half the appeal of camp was getting away from Monica. If she came too, I'd be dodging her the whole time. What if we were put in the same group?

But I couldn't say this to Mama. She'd get that pained look that she always got when we did something wrong. She'd say I was unkind, that I was disappointing her, that I should be nice to my sister. So all I said was, "I don't think she'd like it. She doesn't like horses." I had no idea whether that was true or not.

Mama gave me a funny look, and said she'd think about it and talk to Daddy. Then she went back to loading the dishwasher.

The next day she talked to Samantha's mother and found out how much the camp cost. "Mountain Glen is out, I'm afraid, Erin. It's way too expensive," she told me.

"Aww—what about just for one of us? What if I went and not Monica?"

"I'm sorry, Erin, it's just too much money."

"Just for two weeks? Please?" But this, of course, did not get me anywhere.

So it looked like a pretty dull summer, with a lot of Monica in it. Our family never took real vacations—we couldn't afford them. Aside from an occasional day at the beach and a week of church camp back in the mountains near Asheville, I'd just be hanging around in Shipley. Mama said if I acted bored and grumpy and whiny, she'd send me to Vacation Bible School.

Some vacation.

Chapter 8

Problem Sisters

Mama was canning peaches, and she had me and Monica helping. I complained at first—I was in the middle of a good book—but Mama said she'd pay us. So there I stood at the kitchen table with two big bowls in front of me, one for peach slices and one for the peelings and the pits.

Once I started doing it, I really didn't mind. I liked to see if I could get the whole peel off in one long strip, and I liked the colors inside, the creamy shades of orange and the crimson thready stuff around the pit, and the way half the peach came away from the pit so easily, with only a slight tearing sound. That's why they're called freestones, Mama told us.

"How come in catalogs the color they call peach doesn't

look like a real peach?" I asked, thinking of some clothes I'd been looking at the day before.

"Must be somebody made that up that never saw a peach," said Mama with a grin. She had been cheerful most of the time lately, and it was even kind of fun to do these things at home with her. Not like sometimes, when she'd be all tense and grumpy.

For the summer she'd gotten her hours at the bank reduced, so she was only working eleven to two, when lots of people came to the drive-through during their lunch break. That was one reason she was pretty happy this summer—she said it was less boring when there were lots of customers, plus she could spend more time at home with us or out in the garden.

This was Saturday, and most weeks she only worked Monday through Friday, so she had picked today for canning and making preserves out of all these peaches. It was only a little after nine o'clock and she was well under way. "Got to do this while it's cool," she said. Two big pots were sitting on the stove, one with the electric burner blazing red under it, the other just waiting.

"I'm going to Hannah's at ten," I reminded her. Hannah was the main reason this was an okay summer so far. Some of my other friends were in day camp or sleepaway camp practically all summer, but Hannah didn't go to camp much because her mother was a stay-at-home mom. I was spending a lot of time with her.

"What have you two got planned?" Mama asked.

"Oh, just hanging around. We might go swimming later."

"Mm-hmm." Mama seemed to be concentrating only on the peaches simmering in the pot, but a minute later, as soon as Monica went to the bathroom, she said quietly, "Why don't you and Hannah play here? You always go off and Monica's left all alone."

I could feel nerves and muscles in my face squinch up, and my stomach, too. "Monica bugs us," I said, not looking at Mama, just at a peach pit I was fiddling with. "We want to play *together*, just me and Hannah."

"She wouldn't stay with you and Hannah the whole time." Mama's voice was almost pleading. "It would just be nice for her to have other kids around."

Whatever was squinched up inside me was hardening—mushy guilt turning into something tougher. "We have stuff to do at Hannah's," I said flatly. I tossed the pit into the bowl, picked up the next peach, and started peeling.

Mama sighed and turned back to the stove. "You used to follow her around, when you were a little bitty thing," she said softly, still with her back to me. "Both of you with that wispy, almost blond hair . . . You thought she hung the moon."

I didn't see what that had to do with anything.

When Monica returned, she picked up her knife and took another peach out of the big paper bag. We peeled silently for a few minutes.

Then Mama said, "Monica, why don't you call a friend, too? You could invite somebody over today."

"Naah," said Monica.

"It might be fun," encouraged Mama. "How about Madeline? Or Jennifer—she's a nice girl."

"Don't want to." Typical Monica—no reason, no explanation offered, and you might as well forget about trying to change her mind. Anyway, who would want to hang around with her?

"So what are you going to do all day?" I was careful to keep my voice mildly curious, not critical, but Mama gave me a sharp look.

Monica shrugged. "Read. Play basketball. Can some peaches."

I glanced down. "You could shave your legs." Last Sunday afternoon, when our family went swimming, I was mortified. All the other girls Monica's age had smooth legs, and there was Monica with her lanky legs as hairy as a man's.

True, I didn't shave yet, either, but I was two years younger, and the hair on my legs was a lot thinner and almost blond. Anyway, I wasn't planning to wait much longer.

When we were spreading out our towels, I had said to her, quiet and fierce, "You're the only girl your age who doesn't shave your legs. It looks weird!"

"Oh, you just shut up," was all she said. I kicked off my flip-flops, ran to the pool, and dived deep into clean cool water where I couldn't hear anything at all, where everything I saw—the concrete walls, the moving legs and arms and bright swimsuits—was softened and tinged with blue.

Mama took me to Hannah's house, and as soon as we were out of the driveway I said, "Why does Monica have to be so weird?"

"What do you mean by 'weird'?"

"Well—well," I sputtered—the answer was so obvious that I didn't know where to begin. "She won't shave her legs, and she wears funny clothes sometimes, and she says dumb things—she's just weird."

"You mean she's a little different from most of the girls," Mama said.

"She's a *lot* different."

"I don't know as I'd call that a lot. She doesn't have two heads. She doesn't go to church in pajamas and a cowboy hat."

This was nothing to joke about. "*Mama*," I snapped. "Nobody likes her. She doesn't have any friends."

I saw something in Mama's face then. We were coasting up to a red light, and when the car stopped she turned and looked at me. "I'm worried about that, too, Erin. I'm sorry she embarrasses you, but mostly I'm worried about how lonely she is."

Mama's face was sad. I'd thought she didn't really see the trouble with Monica, but now I knew she'd been thinking about it, too. But after a second I just stared straight ahead at the dashboard. So now I was supposed to feel *sorry* for Monica?

Mama let me out at the end of the driveway. Hannah's house was beautiful, I thought—a big old wooden house, creamy yellow with white trim, with a porch that curved around two sides and a trellis covered with pink roses.

By the time I got to Hannah's door, I wasn't as mad as I had been, but I felt worse. Being just plain mad isn't such a bad thing, really. It's just one pure feeling—you're mad and you know who you're mad at and you know you're right.

But now, ringing Hannah's doorbell, I was stuck with a whole mess of feelings, like storm clouds around my head. I was still mad, but now I felt guilty, too, and even a little sorry for Monica. And maybe it was good that I'd talked to Mama, but I wanted her to feel sorry for *me*, because I had this strange embarrassing sister. But she didn't feel a bit sorry for me. She thought Monica's feelings were more important.

When Hannah opened the door, I was surprised to see that she looked mad, too. She was holding her flute. "I have to practice this stupid thing before we can play. *And* I have to do it in my room by myself. Sorry—you can hang out in the living room and watch TV or something."

"How long do you have to practice?"

"Fifteen more minutes."

Mrs. McLaren poked her head in while I was surfing cartoons. "Hello, Erin. Hannah will be with you in a few minutes. She was supposed to get her practicing done before you came. I'm off to the grocery store." She gave me a quick polite smile and disappeared.

As soon as the sound of Mrs. McLaren's car faded away, the flute sounds from upstairs stopped, too, and a minute later Hannah came in. Probably about five minutes had passed.

"I'm out of jail," she said. "Come on up."

"Was that fifteen minutes?"

"Close enough," she shrugged.

"Did you have a big fight with your mom?" I asked on the way up the pink-carpeted stairs.

"She never never never lets up," Hannah growled. "The whole school year, it was"—she made her voice high and per-snickety—"'Do your homework. Practice your flute. Did you study enough for that test? Why didn't you do better in math?' Now it's summer, and all I hear is 'You need a math tutor. Study that workbook. Practice your flute. Clean your room.'"

"That's so bad," I said. "Is your dad like that, too?"

"Yeah, but not half as much as *her*. Anyway, he's nicer since he moved out. *She* thinks I have to be good at every-thing. Why can't I just be good at soccer?"

We went into Hannah's room, and she closed the door behind us. The room looked like a tornado had come through—clothes all over the floor, dried-up plants in pots on the windowsill, papers and junk scattered over her desk.

"You know what the real problem is?" she said, pacing. "Laura. Miss Perfect. Everything they like, she does it really well. She makes me look bad no matter what I do."

"Well, at least you don't have Monica for a sister," I blurted out. For a second I was surprised at my own words, then I wished I hadn't said anything. *Don't remind people, dummy*, I told myself.

Hannah stopped pacing and looked down at me—I was sitting on her bed. She folded her arms and studied me for a minute, as if seeing me in a new way.

Was she thinking I could turn out as dorky as Monica?

"Yeah," she said slowly. "I guess that's hard, too."

I wanted to jump up and hug her, but I didn't.

"I mean," she said, "Monica's not a bad person or anything, but she's not . . . not what you want a big sister to be."

"She's a dork."

"Well, yeah, kind of."

"What if there's a dork gene and I've got it, too?" I said in a breathless rush.

I was totally serious but Hannah laughed. "There might be a Miss Perfect gene, but I sure didn't get that one." She sat down beside me. "Don't worry, of course you don't have the dork gene."

Then I did hug her. "I guess we both have problem sisters," I said. Everything felt lighter now. And even though I knew deep down that it was a lot worse to have Monica than Laura for a sister, I didn't say it. I liked this new bond between Hannah and me, and I didn't want to spoil it.

So I spelled it out. "You think you're supposed to be like Laura. And I'm afraid I might turn out to be like Monica."

"Right," said Hannah. "Now if we can just figure out who we really are."

Chapter 9

Trespassing

Hannah and I looked at each other. It was like what she'd just said—about figuring out who we really were—was some kind of challenge. A dare.

It wasn't something I said out loud, or even understood completely. But I could feel it. Hannah and I weren't made in the same molds as Laura and Monica, and it was time for us to *prove* we were different. Time to stop acting the way everybody expected us to act.

Somehow I knew Hannah was thinking what I was thinking, and my eyes were shining with the same dare that was in her eyes. We were daring ourselves to do—what?

I had no idea.

"Let's do something," I said. I jumped up from the bed, pushing my hair back restlessly. "Let's go somewhere."

"Like where?"

"I don't know." I felt myself sinking a little. Without someone driving us, there was nowhere interesting to go. "I wish we could drive."

"We could walk to the pool," Hannah said half-heartedly.

"We always do that."

We were quiet for a minute. I kicked off my sandals and clenched my toes in the carpet.

"I know!" Hannah said. "We can go somewhere right here—in the house. *There's nobody else here.*"

I stared at her. I was thinking maybe she was onto something, but I didn't know exactly what. "Where is everybody?"

"Mom's getting groceries, Laura's at her cello lesson, and Jake's off somewhere with his friends. Cool—I like *never* get to be in the house by myself."

"But," I said uncertainly, "it's just your house. I mean, what can we do that's, you know, special?"

"Here's what we can do: we can go in Laura's room."

I grinned back at her. Even though I didn't think it was such a thrill to go in Laura's room, I remembered that a couple of weeks earlier Laura had gotten mad about Hannah borrowing something without asking, and she'd started locking her door all the time. Even if she was in there with the door open, she told Hannah she had to knock first and say "May I come in?" This made Hannah mad as a wet hen, as Mama would say.

"It's probably locked, you know," I warned Hannah.

For answer she walked over to her dresser, opened a drawer, and held up a key.

It was one of those old-fashioned keys with no jagged edges, just a smooth shaft with a handle on one end and a piece of metal like a tiny flag on the other. This made sense because Hannah's house was really old.

"Does that go to Laura's room?"

"I think so. I haven't had a chance to try it yet. I just found it yesterday." She explained that she'd found a bunch of old keys in a box in the attic, four of them just alike. She'd brought down one of them and it worked perfectly in her own door, so she figured that the same key must work for all five bedrooms. Laura must have the fifth key.

We grinned at each other, and three seconds later we were at Laura's door. I tried the knob, and sure enough it was locked. Hannah was so excited she fumbled with the key. "Let me do it," I said impatiently.

"Hey, it's mine," she answered, so I backed off. Then with a little sound like a creaky spring, the key turned, and Hannah pushed the door open.

It was dim inside; the blue-and-white-checked curtains were half closed around the still fan on the windowsill. The bed was made up without the tiniest wrinkle. There was a tall white dresser, a metal music stand, a desk with books and papers neatly stacked.

"She keeps it perfect even though nobody sees it," I whispered, awed. I'd always thought being neat was just so you wouldn't be embarrassed if somebody came to visit.

Hannah started opening drawers, pawing through the stuff on the desk. The clothes in the drawers were all carefully folded and stacked, even the socks, and this gave me an idea. "Let's mix up all her socks. She won't even look for them till fall, and then she'll think she's going crazy." I started pairing a blue sock with a white one, a black with a gray, and carefully refolding them.

Hannah smiled approvingly but wasn't really interested. I had the feeling she was after something more important. She put a Beatles disk in Laura's CD player, an expensive one that no one but Miss Perfect herself was allowed to touch. "Yellow Submarine" filled the room.

"What if your mom comes back? Or Laura?" I worried. "We won't hear them coming."

"Laura's going shopping after her lesson. And my dear mother takes forever at Food Lion, plus—aha!"

"What?" I demanded. Hannah, beside a drawer with sweaters tumbling out, was holding a book with no words on the cover, just a picture of a pink sunset reflected in a lake.

"I knew she had a diary," Hannah said triumphantly. "I heard her telling one of her friends. This is it."

"Let me see."

The title page said:

Diary of Laura Jean McLaren
Shipley, North Carolina
June 1, 2003—

She had filled up about half of the book's lined pages, all in purple ink, in neat (of course) cursive, with big loops and some extra curlicues.

"This is great," Hannah said. "She would absolutely die if she knew I'm reading her diary."

I had a moment's doubt. "Well, it *is* kind of private. I mean, maybe we shouldn't . . ."

"You don't have to, but *I'm* going to. After all the things she's done to me?" Hannah's eyes were fierce. "Anyway, she'll never find out," she said, adding wickedly, "unless I decide to tell her."

She sat down on the bed and started turning the pages slowly, skimming. My sock project suddenly seemed dumb, and I closed the drawer. Then I just stood there for a minute, my hand on the drawer pull. Reading someone's diary was wrong, I was pretty sure of that.

As if she had heard my thoughts, Hannah looked up at me. It was a narrow-eyed look, a sizing-up look. "You wouldn't tell her, would you?"

"No way," I protested. "Of course not."

"Don't you want to know what's in it?" she demanded.

"Well, yeah, but . . ." I looked away, tightening my fingers on the drawer pull.

"Are you on my side or not?"

"Sure I'm on your side, I just—"

"Erin, I'm not like Laura. Don't be a dork like Monica. We're changing things, and we're in this together."

I went limp. Well, I thought, I wasn't searching for the diary, and I didn't find it or open it. I'd just be looking over Hannah's shoulder; she was the one who would really be reading it. I wouldn't even touch it.

I sat down next to her. "Anything good yet?"

Chapter 10

Dear Diary

March 12
Dear Diary,

Andy Sherman followed me around in the halls today. It was so embarrassing! Every time we changed classes I'd go to my locker and there he was.

He adores me—great. Except I can't stand him. He's pathetic. And pimply.

I wish I'd never been nice to him. Marina was smart—the first time or two he tried talking to her, she looked right through him as if nobody was there. He finally took the hint.

Now if it was only you-know-who . . .

Got the math test back—100.

April 7
Dear Diary,

 Today Mrs. Baker said I'm the best student she's had in 20 years! She wants me to concentrate on the Bach for the music festival. I would love to get first place and I'm going to practice really hard. I only have 4 weeks!

 Actually I shouldn't be thrilled. Mrs. Baker's probably had about 5 cello students in her whole life. Cello is not exactly a big thing in Shipley. This is such a dumb little town—I can't wait to get out of here.

Hannah and I were reading to ourselves while Beatles songs poured from the CD player.

"I want to find out who you-know-who is," muttered Hannah, turning a page. "I'm sick of cello lessons and hundreds on math tests."

April 13
Dear Diary,

 Got an A on my paper about A Separate Peace. *It wasn't a great paper but Mrs. Grayson loves me. She'd give me an A no matter what I wrote. Wish Mr. Lowery was like that. I have to get better in chemistry or I'm going to blow my average. If I don't get into a great college with a great music school, I'll just die.*

 Wish Jake and Hannah would shut up. They're downstairs howling about something, The Simpsons *maybe. They always have time to slack off—I never do. It doesn't really matter for them anyway. They'll go to some okay college and have a good time and live in Shipley forever. I want to do better than that. But anyway it's still not fair. I work all the time and they just take it easy.*

"Take it easy! What does she know," Hannah said as "Sgt. Pepper's Lonely Hearts Club Band" faded out. Then, in the second of silence before "With a Little Help From My Friends," I heard the slam of a car door in the driveway.

We jumped up, and Hannah went to put the diary back while I dashed to the CD player. It took me a long minute to find the right button, but finally I saw "power" and hit it. In the sudden quiet I heard someone moving around downstairs.

I glanced around the room, and it looked just the way it did when we entered. We started to tiptoe out, and then Hannah said in a frantic whisper, "The CD! Take it out!" I fumbled the disk out of the machine and into its box, putting the box carefully on the rack.

Hannah locked the door behind us. Then we ran to her room and collapsed on the bed.

"Who's downstairs?" I whispered between giggles.

"Must be Jake. Mama can't be done shopping yet."

A minute later we heard footsteps on the stairs. My heart was still racing. Guiltily I grabbed a book from the table next to the bed and pretended to be reading the back cover. Hannah didn't pretend to do anything; she just leaned back with her hands behind her head and stared out into the hall.

The footsteps reached the top, and the person who stepped into view was not Jake—it was Laura. Hannah and I cracked up.

She rested the cello case on the floor and gave us a disgusted look. "What is *with* you two?"

We just kept giggling, and she went on to her room. We heard the key in the lock, and the door closing.

Hannah gave me a high five. *Partners in crime*, I said to myself, *and we got away with it*.

But there was one thing we'd forgotten.

It was the Fourth of July, and I was sitting on the porch swing, waiting for the long hot afternoon to end so we could go to the picnic and fireworks. Monica was over on the Lovingers' driveway with her basketball. She'd been dribbling and shooting for close to an hour while I read a book, with the thumps of the ball and the rattling of the hoop for background music.

Almost a week had gone by since we'd found Laura's diary. I hadn't looked at it again, but Hannah had, twice. She figured she'd read at least half of it by now. She'd told me what was in it, a lot of boring stuff about school but sometimes some pretty juicy gossip. And she'd found out the identity of Mr. You-Know-Who, but the name didn't mean anything to me since I didn't know that many kids who were going to be juniors in high school. Hannah said he was cute, though.

Hannah and her family would be at the picnic and the fireworks, and so would just about everybody else we knew. It was the same every year—we went to the high-school stadium and spread out a blanket on the field, and had a picnic, and there were two or three bands that took turns playing. The high-school pep band played patriotic songs, and then there was maybe a country-rock band from New Bern or Durham, and maybe a fiddler playing bluegrass.

While the music was going it'd be slowly getting darker and cooler, and the kids would be running around all over the field, and pretty soon there'd be lightning bugs along with the mosquitoes. We'd catch lightning bugs and put them in paper cups that still smelled of lemonade, and we'd clap our hands over the cups and watch the glow through the waxy paper.

By the time it got dark enough for fireworks, it would be almost my bedtime, and I'd sit on the picnic blanket and lean back on Mama or Daddy, and my eyes would half close but I'd still watch the big sparkly bursts and wonder what exactly was raining down in those trails of blue and gold, and whether it ever landed on anyone's head.

"Hey, Miss Erin," Daddy called from inside the house. "Phone's for you." I went inside for the cordless and brought it back to the porch swing, saying hello on the way.

"Erin, you have totally screwed me up." It was Hannah.

I opened my mouth but nothing came out.

"I'm grounded for a whole week, and it's your fault."

"What—what do you mean, my fault?"

"Laura found the socks."

Something inside me sank, fast. I held onto the chain of the swing and slowly sat. "Oh no."

"Oh yes. So right away she figured it had to be me, and she pitched a huge fit, and Mama got into it, and now I'm grounded. For a week. All because of your dumb idea about mixing up her socks."

"Oh no. Hannah, I'm really sorry. Didn't you tell her you didn't do it?"

"Yeah, but they just thought I was lying. So I told them you did it, but they still thought I was lying. They were yelling at me so much, I finally admitted I had a key, and then Mama made me give it to her. So now I can't read the diary ever again."

"Do they know you read it?"

"Not really, but they think I did. Laura kept saying, 'Did you read my diary? Did you? Did you?' And I kept saying no, but then she said I must have because it wasn't exactly where she left it. But that's a lie, I left it under the sweaters where it always is. But of course my parents only believe *her*, they never believe me."

I felt sick inside. I stared at Monica playing basketball, without actually seeing her. "I'm really sorry," I almost whispered. "It was a stupid thing to do."

"Well, you just have fun at the fireworks. I can't go. I can't go anywhere for a whole week. You go have a great time."

She hung up.

At the fireworks, Mama wanted to know what was the matter with me. "Nothing," I said.

I sat with my family and watched an ant climb awkwardly across a tiny gap from a grass blade onto the blanket. I flicked it back onto the grass.

The McLarens came in—Mrs. McLaren, Laura and a friend of hers, and Jake—trooping past us in search of a good place to settle. Mrs. McLaren said hello to my parents, but not to me.

"Where's Hannah tonight?" Mama asked me as they passed.

"Home. Grounded."

"What for?"

I just shrugged, and right then Samantha's mother stopped to talk to Mama, so she didn't ask me any more questions.

Monica had brought her backpack, and when I saw what she was now pulling out of it, I groaned silently. Well, almost silently. She crossed her legs—her *hairy* legs—and began to knit. Half of a blue square hung from one needle like a flag, and click by click she was adding a row.

How weird could you get? Sitting there knitting, like somebody's old grandma, in the middle of the Shipley

Fourth of July picnic. And Mama admiring her stitches, as if there wasn't anything weird about it.

I hunched on the farthest corner of the blanket and tried to become Frodo, hiding from the Black Riders. I pressed myself to the earth, underneath an overhang of rocks and tree roots, my hobbit friends close beside me. But I couldn't feel the shelter—I felt exposed, as if the whole world was looking at the back of my neck, and my friends kept slipping away. I stared at my knees and waited for dark.

Chapter 11

Hoops

I was sitting on the front porch swing one evening after dinner, reading *The Fellowship of the Ring* for the second time, when Gary and Russell Lovinger came out of their house. They didn't say a word to each other. Gary, the older one—he was going to be a senior—just got in his car and roared out of the driveway.

"Wish I had a car," said Monica. She was sitting in a chair on the far side of the porch, doing her stupid knitting, except now she was watching Gary's bright blue Dodge Neon disappearing around the corner.

"You can't drive for three more years," I said.

"Two. You can get a learner's permit when you're fifteen."

I didn't answer, just watched Russell fooling around with a basketball in the now-empty driveway. He dribbled toward the hoop and did a layup that missed.

Monica put her knitting in a bag and went down the front steps and over to the edge of the Lovingers' driveway. *Oh, great,* I thought, *she's gonna pester Russell.* Russell and Gary never had much time for us. They usually didn't even say hi.

But Monica didn't say anything, just stood there watching as he dribbled and took shots and chased the ball. As he dashed past her I noticed that she was as tall as he was, even though he was two years older.

She must want to play, I thought, but she stood there with her hands behind her back like a five-year-old who's too shy to join the party. What a dork.

Russell didn't seem to know she was there. But then he missed a rebound, and the ball took a weird bounce and rolled toward Monica, who picked it up.

She bounced the ball a few times and looked at the basket. She was way too far back, but she didn't move up. She just raised the ball and took a shot. *Swish.*

I think my mouth dropped open. I know Russell's did. "Hey, nice shot!" he said, and then he went for the ball and passed it back to her.

Over and over she sent the ball flying, from up close and far back, and she hardly ever missed. Mama came out on the porch and stood watching, arms folded. My book lay closed on my lap, and nobody said a word.

After a while Russell looked at his watch and said, "I gotta go. I'm supposed to mow the lawn over at my grand-mama's house." He took a shot that bounced off the rim, and as Monica recovered the ball he said, "Girl, you are *good*. Play me a little one-on-one sometime?"

All of a sudden she looked awkward again, and stared down at the ball in her hands. "Okay." Her face was flushed and she seemed to be fighting back a smile.

The next morning I was reading on the couch, still in paja-mas, hadn't even had breakfast yet, when I heard Mama and Monica going out the front door. *Hey*, I thought, *they didn't tell me they were going anywhere*. I went to the window.

They were out in the Lovingers' driveway with a bas-ketball, and Mama was pointing and explaining something, and then they were doing some kind of drill, passing the ball back and forth, zigzagging down the driveway toward the basket.

Mama played basketball back when she was in high school, I remembered. She never played after that, but she was a big Carolina fan. One of her coworkers gave her a bumper sticker that said IF GOD ISN'T A TARHEEL, WHY IS THE SKY CAROLINA BLUE? She put it on the bulletin board next to our refrigerator. And when Duke played Carolina on TV, forget it—the house could be on fire and she wouldn't notice.

I watched them for a few more minutes before going back to my book. They looked like they were having a great time. Mama was calling out advice and praising every good pass Monica made, and the look on Monica's face was one I'd hardly ever seen, really absorbed and focused and happy.

Mama never offered to teach *me* basketball.

Every time I thought of Hannah it was like bumping an already-sore toe. Why did I have to be so stupid? And when would Hannah ever forgive me? Probably I could have called her—I don't think her parents would have kept her from talking on the phone. But I didn't call.

A few times I played with another friend, but there weren't that many kids around. I'd started depending on Hannah a lot, and now she wasn't talking to me.

I'd hang around the house in the morning, playing a computer game or something, maybe helping Mama in the yard if she asked. Then she'd go off for her three-hour shift at the bank, and it would just be me and Monica.

Monica would hang out with the guinea pigs or else she'd turn on the TV and do her knitting in front of the soaps. Sometimes I'd play the piano, and Monica would complain that she couldn't hear the TV, and then I'd play louder for a minute before going softer.

She practiced basketball almost every day, usually in the morning or evening when it wasn't so hot. Mostly she played by herself, but sometimes with Russell or Mama or me. But I didn't like to play too often. It wasn't really fair; she was so much taller than me. And better.

One day I called Samantha, figuring that she must be back from camp by now, and she was—she'd just gotten home the day before. She told me about Mountain Glen and riding horses and canoeing, and I kept saying "cool" and wishing I didn't feel so jealous. She never asked anything about me.

I asked her to come over, but she said she'd promised to spend the whole day with her mom, since she'd been away so long.

"Tomorrow maybe?" I asked.

"Maybe. I'll call you, okay? Maybe tomorrow or the next day."

I flopped on my bed and started reading a book, but I felt restless, and I was glad when Mama finally got home.

"Will you take me to the mall?" I asked as soon as she came in.

"Give me a minute, okay?" she said. She'd brought in the mail and was glancing through a pile of envelopes and magazines. "What do you want at the mall?"

"I don't know . . . I could use some new shorts."

"Well, I do need a couple of things myself. Okay, just a minute." She went to the living room and called over the TV noise, "Monica, would you like to go to the mall?"

I groaned. "Does she have to come too?"

Mama whipped around. "Erin, if you can't be polite, you're not going anywhere."

"Okay, okay," I muttered.

An hour later, just as the three of us were coming out of the drugstore at the mall, I almost collided with Samantha and Kayla.

"Hey," I said to Samantha. "I thought you had to stay home with your mom."

"Oh—uh—yeah, most of the day I do. I just wanted to make a really quick trip to the mall." She looked totally embarrassed. "I had to get some things," she added.

"Oh."

Kayla tossed her hair and tugged on Samantha's arm. "Come on, Sam, we've got things to do."

Samantha gave me a little smile and wave, and the two of them walked off.

Great. Obviously Samantha just made up an excuse because she didn't want to play with me. First I lost Kayla as a friend, then I lost Hannah, and now Samantha. I was running out of friends to lose.

Chapter 12

Following Hannah

One Sunday afternoon, hanging around the house, I put my hand on the phone three or four times, thinking I'd finally call Hannah. And then I thought of her bitter voice saying "You go have a great time," and I took my hand off the phone.

Mama told me to water the plants on the porch, so I was dousing a geranium when the phone rang, and it was Hannah herself. My heart rose—maybe even *leaped*—at the sound of her voice.

"Do you want to, maybe, do something today?" She sounded hesitant, and that surprised me.

"Sure," I said. "How about you come over?"

"Okay, great. So . . . you're not mad at me?"

"I thought *you* were mad at *me*."

"Well, just at first. But I was so, like, nasty to you on the phone, when I called you on the Fourth."

"But it was my fault you got in trouble," I answered.

"But still, we were both in Laura's room, and I shouldn't have blamed everything on you. I'm sorry I talked to you in that mean way."

"Well, I'm sorry about my stupid idea about the socks."

"That's okay. When should I come over?"

"Right now!"

"Put your dollar here, honey," the bus driver said when I held it out to her. She pointed to a glass box with a hole in the top. "That's right, honey."

I was riding a county bus for the first time since moving to Shipley. Hannah and I plopped down in the hard blue plastic seats and looked at everything. From up here even the familiar streets looked different. There were only three other people on the bus when we boarded, but lots more got on as we crept along, stopping and starting. Most of them were black people. The only one I recognized was a crazy old man who was always sitting on a bench downtown. He held a brown paper bag on his lap and muttered to himself.

It was Hannah's first time on the bus, too. She was the one who found out where you could catch a bus to go to the mall. She showed up at my house with a plan, and Mama said okay. Hannah didn't even ask her mother if she could go. "She knows I came over to your house," Hannah shrugged. "That's all she needs to know."

We went everywhere at the mall. We looked at music, movies, stationery, makeup, and clothes clothes clothes. On Mama's orders we stopped in Stockdale's, just long enough to say hi to Daddy and check in with Mama by phone. Then we looked in the arcade and said hi to Ricky and Jesse from school, who were busy shooting things on video screens. We ate hamburgers at the food court. We fingered things in practically every store. And we both bought short, glittery tops that would show our bellies, and that we knew our mothers would absolutely hate.

Mine was purple and Hannah's was blue, and the style and color were just different enough that we wouldn't look like twins. Buying it took all but a dollar of the allowance money I'd been saving, but I didn't care. Hannah and I looked at each other in the dressing-room mirrors, and we looked sexy and older and really cool. Kayla was allowed to wear clothes like this, but most of us weren't.

"My mama will blow the roof off," said Hannah with deep satisfaction.

I grinned back at her. "So will mine."

As it turned out, Mama was pretty calm about it. She was in the kitchen when I got home, and as soon as I walked in she asked me what I'd bought. I tried not to look nervous when I opened the bag.

Mama held the top up against me and shook her head. "Erin, you *know* I don't approve of little girls wearing things like that, and neither does your daddy."

"I'm not a little girl! Anyway, what's wrong with it?"

"It looks cheap."

"Well, it wasn't. It cost twenty dollars."

Mama sighed. "I don't mean that kind of cheap, Erin. I mean trashy. It makes *you* look cheap."

"How can I look cheap? I don't have a price tag."

Mama glared. "Don't you smart off to me, young lady."

I shrugged, and opened a drawer to get scissors. Then I just stood there holding them for a long minute while Mama and I stared at each other. Finally she gave a big sigh and said, "Well, I guess you have to do a few things on your own now. And you did buy it with your own money. I'll let you keep it, but you are *not* going to wear that to school. Is that clear?"

"Sure," I said, and clipped the tags.

I grinned to myself. I'd gotten off easy.

When Daddy came home after work, he looked at me in my purple top and said, "What the heck is that?"

"It's my new top," I said, miffed. Naturally, he wouldn't have a clue about what was in style.

"Well, you better take it back to the store. It's missing a piece."

"Ha-ha."

"Sue, you let this little girl go around like that?" he called up the stairs.

"I'm not a little girl," I hollered before Mama could answer him.

He went upstairs and I stomped out to the backyard, where Monica was setting up the grill.

"I knew Daddy'd have something to say about that outfit," she said.

"So? I still get to keep it."

I sat on the back steps and watched her putting in the charcoal. She was really getting tall and skinny. I looked down at my stomach and legs. I was definitely not fat, no one could call me fat. But my bare belly did stick out just a little over the waistband of my shorts, now that I was sitting down. Oh sugar, maybe I shouldn't have bought the top. But it did look good in the store mirror, I knew it did. I'd just have to be careful and not eat too much.

That night Hannah called and told me that her mother had a fit about the top. "She said I had to return it. But I told her I lost the receipt, so I couldn't."

"Did you really lose it?"

"No way. I just put it in the garbage. I crumpled it up and buried it under a lot of chicken bones."

"Yucky," I said. "But smart. Your mom's not going to search through that."

"Right. But she won't let me wear the top—ever. For the rest of the summer she'll be watching me every minute. I'll get her back, though. You know what I'm going to do?"

"What?"

"I'm going to wear it to school the very first day."

"How can you get away with that?"

"I'll just wear another shirt over it, and take it off the minute I get to school."

"Awesome. Hannah, you are so smart. I'm going to do it, too."

It was great to hang around with Hannah again. We did a lot of the same things we used to—went swimming, or kicked a soccer ball around the backyard, or made jewelry with beads—but something about her was different now. She made a lot of sarcastic comments about people, especially her parents and Laura and a few of the kids at school. She was tougher, even a little mean, but never to me. We were a team, and we'd always stick together. I knew that, and I was sure she knew it, too. It didn't have to be said out loud.

Hannah, Jake, Laura, and their mom would be leaving on vacation soon—a long one, to California. I hated to think about three whole weeks without Hannah. And if I couldn't be with her, I wished my family could go on vacation to Disneyland or some other special place, instead of just spending a day at the beach now and then.

Every Sunday at church I saw Kayla, with the Shadow by her side. The Shadow was what Hannah called Danielle. And usually you could find Jane-Marie and Samantha trailing along, too. None of them had anything to say to me, beyond a bored hi. And once I heard Kayla say something about Monica's dress, and the rest of her groupies snickered.

"What is so great about Kayla?" I demanded. It was a Sunday afternoon, and Hannah and I were sitting in the grass in her backyard. "Now Samantha and Jane-Marie follow her around just like Danielle."

"Kayla *is* great," said Hannah. "If you like prissy little blond airheads."

I was picking stalks of clover and pulling the leaves off. "*You* know she's a prissy little airhead and *I* know she's a prissy little airhead. But why don't *they* know it?"

"It's the look, Erin. Don't you see? She wears shiny little skirts and a ton of makeup, and she has long blond hair that she brushes all the time so everybody will notice it." Hannah mimicked Kayla tossing her head as she pulled an imaginary brush through her hair.

"Plus," she went on, flopping down on her stomach in the grass, "she has more CDs and more clothes than anybody in the whole school, and she goes skiing in Colorado for vacations. That stuff makes her, like, *sooo* cool."

"She used to be my friend," I said. "Now she's so snooty she barely says hello. And Jane-Marie and Samantha were my friends too, not like heart-to-heart, but they were friendly. And now they don't talk to me either. I bet Kayla told them not to."

Hannah suddenly rolled over, sat up, and looked me in the eye. "*Let's get her.*"

I was startled. "What do you mean?"

"Get Kayla. Pay her back." Hannah looked like this was something she'd been dying to do for her whole life, and now the moment had come. She was so intense, I was almost scared.

"Maybe," I said slowly.

"You said you'd get her back. Remember? That day you were on the swing?"

"Yeah, I know. But I never could think of a good way to do it. And anyway, she has all these friends. They'd hate me."

"So?" said Hannah. "You've got me. And I've got an idea."

Chapter 13

In the Middle of the Night

Hannah and I talked it over, again and again. I was the one with doubts; she dismissed them all. Finally I asked her something that had been in the back of my mind for a while. "How come you're so excited about getting Kayla? She's never done anything to you."

"She's stuck-up," said Hannah. "She thinks she's better than everybody else. Besides, she's mean to you, and you're my best friend."

Right then I knew I'd go along with whatever plan Hannah wanted. Hannah, who liked everybody and everybody liked her, who had so many friends she never needed a best one—Hannah McLaren had named *me* her best friend.

I was glowing. So what if Kayla thought I was dorky like Monica? So what if Danielle and Jane-Marie and Samantha wouldn't talk to me, and followed Kayla around like slaves? Hannah and I were best friends.

I still wanted revenge on Kayla. Before, though, I'd wanted it because she made me feel like a worm. Now I wanted it because she deserved it, and because Hannah and I could do it together.

I can't believe we're doing this, I kept thinking as I lay in bed Friday night, staring at the blue lighted numbers on my clock. *I can't believe it.*

Because this was so outrageous, it was like nothing else I'd ever done in my life.

I lay on my back with the sheet up to my chin. The streetlight, shining in my window, made a shadow grid on the opposite wall, and in the center square was the shadow of the little origami bird that hung in the window. The bird shadow floated, turning slowly, always within its shadow cage.

I watched the blue numbers until finally, after an eternity, they said 11:45. Heart hammering, I got out of bed, took off my pajamas, and put on shorts and a T-shirt and sneakers. In the doorway of my bedroom I paused and listened, hearing nothing but the soft whir of the air-conditioning. Then I crept down the carpeted hall to the front door.

I turned the latch of the dead bolt with excruciating

slowness, but it still sounded horribly loud. Then, more quietly, I turned the knob, slipped through, and shut the door behind me.

Stepping into the hot muggy night was like hitting a wall. I set off down the street, grateful for every streetlight, jumping at shadows and, once, at a lazy bark from the old dog who lived four houses down. "Hush, Fred," I said to him, and my voice sounded small and shaky. His house was dark, but I hurried on by in case someone looked out.

All around me the cicadas kept up their crazy noise, as if a million tiny robotic aliens had descended from a spaceship and hidden themselves in the trees and shrubs, and were now chanting some mysterious message that no human could understand.

I was sweating, and there was a cold, hard knot in my stomach in spite of the heat. I tried to make myself Frodo, resolutely traveling toward Mordor, the thick air wrapping me like a cloak. But this only made me think of Black Riders sniffing out their prey, and creepy Gollum sneaking and spying. I was all alone on the street in the middle of the night. What if some scary stranger showed up? What if some neighbor who couldn't sleep looked out their window and saw me and called my parents?

I wanted to go home, but I couldn't. Hannah was waiting for me.

I kept darting glances all around, fearing that I wouldn't hear approaching footsteps, with all the cicada noise and the hum of air conditioners and fans from every house. I turned onto Butler Street, and instantly I saw a car turning onto it, too, turning from the next side street toward me, a little orange light glowing on the side near the headlights, which swept a wide path and any second—I jumped for the nearest bushes. Crouching, I waited till the car was well past me, then emerged and kept walking.

Finally I saw Kayla's house ahead. In this neighborhood you could walk down the street and not even hear the air conditioners, because all the houses were big and far back from the street, in the middle of huge yards. Kayla's street was called Woodland Way, even though there weren't any woods.

Not a single light showed in Kayla's house, except the carriage light on a post at the end of the driveway. But I wasn't going in the driveway. I looked at my watch, and it was five minutes past midnight. I hurried to the corner of Kayla's yard where the big old weeping willow stood with its branches dangling almost to the ground. Pushing them aside, I stepped from the dark night into the even darker shadows of the tree. "Hannah?" I whispered.

No one was there.

I almost panicked. I was five minutes late, six by now. What if she'd gotten tired of waiting for me and left? I looked wildly around the willow's branches and their trembling shadows, and beyond them to the street. Nothing.

What if she wasn't coming at all? She could have fallen

asleep, or chickened out. She could have gotten caught sneaking out of the house.

I began to hope she wouldn't come, because then I could go home and this would all be over. I'd give her five more minutes, I decided. Or maybe four. But as soon as I thought that, a small figure appeared in the street, running.

"Oh my God, I thought you might have given up and gone home," she gasped as soon as she was under the tree. "I was just about to leave and then Jake got out of bed and went down to the kitchen. He ate this humongous bowl of Cheerios. It took him like forever, and if I went downstairs he would've seen me, so I had to wait till he went back to bed."

I nodded, and then we both just looked at each other in the dim, speckled light that came through the leaves. Hannah was still breathing hard from running, and I was breathing hard from terror. I wanted to say, "Hannah, I can't do it. I'm scared and I just can't." The words were dry in the back of my throat, and though I opened my mouth, they wouldn't come out.

Then Hannah patted the backpack that hung from her shoulder and said, "I've got everything right here. Come on, let's do it."

The words died in my throat and settled, deadweight in the pit of my stomach. And I followed Hannah across the dark lawn.

Later I would wish I'd managed to get those words out. I'd wish that Hannah would have listened. And I'd wish that both of us had turned around and gone home. But then it seemed that once we left the shelter of the willow and started across the lawn, there was no way to turn back.

We walked softly around the side of Kayla's house and paused behind a big bush to survey the backyard. Right in the middle was exactly what we'd expected to see—a tent. And a few feet away was something we hadn't expected at all—another tent.

I looked at Hannah in dismay.

"She said she'd sleep out with her cousin," she whispered. "I thought it was just one cousin."

"Which one is she in?" I whispered back.

"How would I know? We'll just have to look."

"Not both of us," I said quickly. "One would be quieter."

"Okay," said Hannah. "I'll find out where she is, and you can do the deed."

I gulped and said stupidly, "Me?"

"Who did you think was going to do it? This is *your* revenge. I'm just the planner. And now the scout."

I hoped my face was as hard to see as hers. When I didn't say anything else, she muttered, "Wait here," set her backpack on the grass, and tiptoed toward the tents.

Holding my breath, I watched her lift the flap of one tent slightly, then a little more. After a moment she lowered it and moved toward the other tent. She must have tripped over a rope or a stake, because all at once she thumped down on one knee. She froze, but there was no sound from the tents, and after a minute she crept to the second tent and peered in.

She came back shaking her head. "It's too dark in there. I'll have to use a light." Slowly she unzipped the backpack, both of us wincing at the sound, and pulled out a flashlight.

"You'll wake them up," I said in a panic.

"Chill out, Erin. I'll put my hand over it."

This was taking forever. Squeezing my hands together again and again, I wished it was all over.

Then Hannah was back. "That one." She pointed to the nearer tent. "She's on the right side."

I stared at the tent, at the triangular flap that concealed Kayla. Hannah reached into the backpack and handed me a pair of scissors.

"I don't know," I said in a shaky whisper. "I don't think I can do it."

For a second I thought Hannah looked frightened, too, but then she said fiercely, "Come on. You have to."

"I don't know," I repeated, turning and turning the scissors in my hands.

"She treats you like dirt. She makes fun of your sister and you too. She thinks she's like the coolest girl in North Carolina."

I just stood there shaking.

"We planned this together, Erin. You and me. We're not gonna be sweet little goody-goodies—we're changing things around here."

Slowly I nodded, watching her determined face in the moonlight. I gripped the scissors and turned toward the tent.

"Go, girl," Hannah said. "Pay her back."

And I walked to the tent, knelt, lifted the flap, unzipped the mosquito net, and cut off Kayla's hair.

The scissors made a slight crunching noise, closing two or three times on that thick hair before Kayla moved her head and made a little sound. I ran as hard as I could, back to the bushes at the side of the house. I thrust the scissors at Hannah, desperate to get them out of my hands. Then we both ran for the street.

There we paused and listened. No screams, not a sound from the Mortons' yard. Hannah put the scissors into her backpack. "You did it," she grinned. "You really did it."

I think I managed to grin back. But all I said was, "I have to get home quick." I ran all the way to my own driveway, and a minute later I was lying rigid in the bed. Triumph and guilt were both roaring through my veins. It was a long time before I got to sleep.

Chapter 14

After

When I woke up it was past ten o'clock. For a minute I gazed drowsily at the clock and the light coming through my white curtains, and then a jolt went through me as I remembered. I scrambled out of bed and realized I was still wearing the same clothes I'd gone out in last night. Nobody except Hannah had seen me in them, but I wrenched them off as if they were contaminated. I dressed hurriedly in fresh clothes and went to the kitchen, hoping Mama wouldn't notice that I'd slept two hours later than usual.

She was on the phone—talking to one of her friends, it sounded like—and she gave me a smile and a wave as I passed through to the living room. I didn't want breakfast. I sat on the couch and picked up a magazine, but I turned the pages without taking anything in.

Hannah and I together had done something—something *daring*, that was the word. Something nobody in the world could ever imagine we'd do. Something that took skill and nerve and stealth. We'd been as brave as Frodo and Sam venturing into Mordor.

Although, I couldn't help thinking uneasily, our cause wasn't quite so noble.

I heard the front door open and close, and then Monica came into the living room, cradling a basketball.

"Well, look who finally got up," she said, plopping into a chair.

"What's wrong with sleeping late once in a while?" I snapped.

For a minute she said nothing, and I pretended to read. Then all the wrong things happened right on top of each other.

With one ear I heard Mama saying one of her long good-byes—"Well, I better get going, Katie . . . I'll see you real soon . . . you be good . . . bye now."

With the other ear I heard Monica say, "I know why you slept late."

I looked at her with a cold rock in the middle of my stomach. Before I could say a word Mama walked in, just as Monica said, "You went somewhere in the middle of the night. I heard you."

Mama stopped in her tracks, beside one end of the coffee table that separated me on the couch from Monica in her chair. She looked at me and said, very slowly, "You did what?"

"Nothing," I said quickly. I shot a furious glance at Monica, expecting her to be smug and triumphant, but mostly she looked confused.

Mama looked from me to Monica. "You heard Erin go outside in the middle of the night?"

Monica nodded silently, her eyes on the basketball in her lap.

"Did you hear her come back in?"

"Yeah."

"What time was this?"

Monica seemed more and more uncomfortable, pressing her fingers against the basketball's unyielding surface, but she answered without hesitating. "She went out about a quarter to twelve, and she came back about twelve-thirty."

Mama looked stunned as she turned to me. "Where did you go?"

"Just—just out walking around. I wanted to, you know, see what it was like. Outside, at night."

"By yourself?"

"Look, I know it was a crazy idea," I said, trying to sound as reasonable as possible. "I just—couldn't sleep and I thought I'd see what it was like outside."

Mama folded her arms. "Erin, I want to know exactly where you went."

"Just around the neighborhood. You know, like around our block and over on Henry Street, and Butler Street, a little."

Her voice was steely-quiet. "Are you sure you didn't go to Kayla Morton's backyard?"

The bottom dropped out of my stomach, and I stared at her without a word.

"Katie Meecham just told me about it on the phone."

"Go ahead," said Mama. "Ring the doorbell."

I watched my hand like it was someone else's, rising slowly, index finger extending to push the white button in the middle of a ceramic plaque painted with violets. Before the chimes died away, the door was flung open, and there stood Mrs. Morton. She was dressed up as always, in a pale pink suit and pearls, with lots of makeup and nail polish, and her hair in smooth, stiff waves. But there was a fretful look on her face, and her automatic smile on seeing us looked strained.

"My daughter has something to say to your daughter," said Mama grimly.

"Oh, really?" said Mrs. Morton vaguely. Then she realized, and stared at me. "You didn't . . . Why you little . . ."

I shrank back a step toward Mama as the distracted look on Mrs. Morton's face mobilized into outrage. "You—Erin Chaney, we had you in our *home*, you were supposed to be Kayla's *friend*. You—" She took a breath. "Listen here, you certainly do have something to say to Kayla, and when you're done I'll have something to say to my lawyer. I'm going to sue your parents for what you did. That's assault, young lady, personal assault."

She stopped and stared at me for a long moment. I didn't dare look at Mama, though I could almost feel how she'd gone rigid, standing just behind my right shoulder.

Mrs. Morton turned and yelled up the stairs, "Ted! Ted!"

"What? What is it?" we heard from upstairs.

"Bring Kayla down here."

In a moment Kayla hurried downstairs with her father close behind. Her face was red and puffy, and when she saw me she twisted what was left of her hair behind her, but not before I saw how ragged it was, up to her chin on one side but a couple of chunks still their full length.

She stopped in front of me and stared. Nobody had to tell her why I was there. "I hate you," she whispered. "I'm going to hate you the rest of my life."

"Erin," Mama prodded in a shaky voice, "what do you have to say?"

"I'm sorry," I said, and didn't know whether I meant it or not, only that I wanted to get away from this terrible scene.

"I've brought a check," said Mama. "To pay for a—a haircut." She gave it to Mrs. Morton, who held it with her fingertips as if it were dirty. "Erin will pay me back out of her allowance."

"Oh, you'll pay all right," Mrs. Morton breathed. "When my lawyer gets done with you, you'll pay."

"Jeannie, now slow down a minute," said Mr. Morton, his fingers lightly touching her sleeve. He had thin, stooped shoulders, and seemed old for a dad. He collected fancy models of antique cars.

Mrs. Morton ignored him. "You'll hear from him on Monday. If not sooner."

When Mama and I got home from the Mortons', she told me in a low voice to stay in my room. Then she sank into a dining-room chair and bent her head, with one hand to her forehead, eyes closed.

I went to my room and lay on the bed, staring at the scattering of glow-in-the-dark stars stuck to the ceiling, barely visible by day. It was almost noon, not even half a day after I'd done it.

What I had imagined would happen in the weeks afterward was this: Every last resident of Shipley would be talking about the mystery. Who on earth could have done it? How did they, or he, or she approach so silently, like an Indian hunter, like one of Tolkien's elves in the forests of Rivendell? Kayla had not even awakened, and whoever it was had escaped.

I'd imagined people shaking their heads in admiration for the unknown assailant, secretly wishing they'd done it themselves. Because, after all, everyone knew she deserved it—Kayla Morton was a mean, stuck-up girl, and so vain about that long golden hair.

I'd imagined Kayla upset, then subdued, humbled.

She'd absentmindedly toss her head, but no golden rippling sheet would fly out. She'd start to brush, the way she used to, about a hundred times a day, but the bristles would scrape her bare neck. She'd realize she was nobody special after all—she could be put down, just as she put other people down. Samantha and Jane-Marie and Danielle would pity her, but they wouldn't be under her spell anymore. They'd realize that there were cooler people to hang around with. Like Erin or Hannah, for instance.

I'd imagined Hannah and me sharing this tremendous secret, gloating when we were alone, and exchanging discreet, knowing glances when we heard others talking about the mystery. I'd imagined Hannah proud of me for proving that I was as daring as she was.

Though I'd been terrified of getting caught in the act, I had never once imagined getting away with it only to get caught the very next day. I hadn't imagined the humiliation of apologizing, or the twisting of my insides when Mrs. Morton yelled at me, or the guilt and fear that gripped me now. What would Mama and Daddy say if the Mortons really sued them? They would hate me. We would be poor, and it would be all my fault.

And one more thing I had never imagined: that my own sister would turn me in. I looked at the wall between our rooms and wished it was as solid and dense as the battlements of Helm's Deep.

I would never have told on Hannah, not in a million years. I thought of Aragorn, folding the ring into Frodo's hand, looking into his eyes and saying, "I would have gone with you into the very fires of Mordor." That's what I would have done for Hannah.

That long day, no matter how many times Mama said, "Was anyone else in on this?" or "What on earth were you thinking?" I always said I did it alone. I said that Kayla had been mean to me for a long time and made fun of me and Monica. I said she was the most conceited girl I'd ever met. I said maybe I did a bad thing but she deserved what she got. Once Mama narrowed her eyes at me and said, "Did Hannah McLaren have something to do with this?" I said no.

Mama and Monica and I had a late and almost silent lunch, with Mama tense and banging her iced-tea glass every time she set it down, and me glaring at Monica, and nobody eating much. I put the dishes in the dishwasher without being told, and then Mama said, "I want you in your room for the rest of the afternoon. No TV, no phone calls. I want you where you can't get into any more trouble."

It wasn't supposed to turn out this way, I kept thinking as I scuffed around my small room, from the window to the dresser to the closet, flopping on the bed and getting up again. I couldn't even feel triumph at the thought of Kayla's miserable face and destroyed hair. I wanted to talk to Hannah, tell her how I felt, hear her say how much Kayla deserved it and how brave I'd been and how she and I would always stick together. But even if I'd been allowed to make phone calls, I couldn't call Hannah. She and her family had left at six that morning for the Raleigh-Durham airport, to catch a plane to California.

By now she was at least halfway across the whole continent of North America. She was probably up in the sky somewhere, above the clouds, starting off on a nice vacation. While I was a prisoner in my little cell.

Chapter 15

What I'd Done

By the time I went to bed on Saturday night, exhausted, I had written Kayla a letter of apology and mailed it. I had turned over to Mama all the money in my purse plus five weeks' worth of future allowances to pay for a hairdresser to even out the mess I'd made. Mama and Daddy had told me I wasn't allowed to go anywhere except to church or on errands with one of them for the next two weeks.

On Sunday morning the last thing I wanted to do was go to Sunday school and church, but nobody gave me a choice.

As soon as I walked in, Ricky Talmadge grinned and made scissor motions with his fingers. Jesse Miller clapped his hands over his buzz cut and said, "No! Don't let her near my beautiful hair!"

And of course, Kayla was there, with her golden hair trimmed short. Danielle and Samantha and Jane-Marie surrounded her protectively, and they all looked at me like I was a rabid raccoon that had somehow wandered into Sunday school. They huddled together and sent wide-eyed, shifting glances my way. Even Shakara seemed half afraid of me.

So I stood around clutching my purse until it was time to move into classrooms, and there I sat very still and tried to concentrate on what the teacher was saying. I didn't look at anybody during class, least of all at Kayla.

The teacher was Mrs. Oakes, whose three children were grown up. She had very tightly curled gray hair and smiled a lot without actually seeming to like us. Samantha's mother had told her that Mrs. Oakes got talked into teaching the sixth-grade group; everyone else the committee asked had flat-out refused.

I wasn't sure if she knew about what I'd done. But the lesson was all about leaving vengeance to the Lord and turning the other cheek.

On Monday there were afternoon thunderstorms, and that evening dark came early. Daddy was on the couch after dinner, reading *U.S. News* magazine, when I wandered into the living room. "Turn on the light for me, will you, hon?" he said without looking up. I went over to the floor lamp in back of him and turned the switch two clicks, and pale yellow light spread through the room.

He kept reading and didn't say thank you. I stood uncertainly for a minute, then sat down at the other end of the couch and tucked my feet under me. "Daddy," I said.

"Hmm?"

I gulped. "Are—are the Mortons going to sue us?"

He finally looked at me. "I sure hope not."

"Well, Mrs. Morton said we'd hear from her lawyer today."

He shook his head. "Not a word so far."

"What if we do hear from them? Will they take a lot of money from us?"

"That all depends. They could take us to court, which would mean we'd have to hire a lawyer, for a phenomenal fee. Or we could settle it out of court—pay the Mortons something to drop the whole thing." He laid the magazine on the floor and folded his arms, looking hard at me. "Could be one heck of a mess."

"I'm sorry," I said. "I never thought—"

"I know, you never thought. Period."

"I'll try to earn some money," I said miserably, wondering how I could do that.

"I had a talk with Ted today—stopped by his office," he said. "He wouldn't come right out and say what they were going to do. But I apologized for your behavior, and he was listening. I figure he's not the type to sue."

"Yeah, but Mrs. Morton wants to."

"Jeannie's got a short fuse. It wouldn't be the first time she's sued somebody, either. But if she has time to cool off, she might see there's no point in it. Even if she gets money—which is not guaranteed—it won't put the hair back on Kayla's head."

I felt a little more hopeful then, but only for a minute. Because Daddy frowned and said, "On the other hand, she just *might* be mad enough to do it anyway, and she just *might* get a big chunk of money out of us. So before you do a fool thing like that again, give a little thought to what you might get your whole family into."

In the grocery store on Thursday, Mama sent me to get cereal while she picked through the green beans and peppers and tomatoes, and the instant I turned down the cereal aisle I came face-to-face with Mrs. Winsted, my fifth-grade teacher. She was putting a box of Grape-Nuts into her cart, and her blond hair was extra frizzy, like she'd just permed it, and she was wearing a tank top and blue-jean shorts that she was a little too fat for.

I was tongue-tied. Mrs. Winsted always dressed up for school, and it was almost like seeing someone naked, to see her in these sloppy summer clothes, behind a cart full of hamburger meat and Marshmallow Pinwheels and Diet Pepsi and a pink toilet brush.

She looked a little startled herself, but she still had the

same cool, firm voice. "Erin, how nice to see you. How's your summer going?"

"Um, it's going okay." I glanced off toward the Corn Chex and Rice Chex.

"Well, from what I hear, you've made quite a name for yourself." I looked nervously back at her and was surprised to see that she looked more amused than disapproving, which set her apart from just about everyone else I'd seen lately.

"I guess so," I said.

But of course Mrs. Winsted couldn't help acting like a teacher. "Really now, Erin, whatever possessed you to do such a thing?"

"I don't know," I mumbled.

"You were never a troublemaker. This doesn't sound to me like something you'd come up with on your own."

She paused, and when I said nothing, she gave me the old I-mean-business look. "You think about it, okay, Erin? Think about who your real friends are."

I just nodded.

Mrs. Winsted's face softened into a smile. "Have a good summer," she said cheerfully. Then she swung her cart around me and turned the corner.

I *was* thinking about it, but not the way she wanted me to. Maybe the whole thing had been Hannah's idea; maybe she'd even persuaded me to do it. But that was only because she was on my side, against mean Kayla and her stupid pals. Hannah was my best friend. Maybe my only friend.

Chapter 16

Grounded

Whap whap whap whap. It was the second Sunday after I'd cut off Kayla's hair. Mama and Daddy were having breakfast and reading the newspaper on the back porch, and I was sitting on the porch steps making about my fiftieth lanyard out of plastic cord.

"Can't a fellow get a little peace and quiet on a Sunday morning?" Daddy said, putting down the sports section.

"Oh, let her do it," Mama said. "The Lovingers aren't home; they went to Gatlinburg."

"Well, don't let her wear out her welcome over there."

Mama turned her coffee cup thoughtfully in her hands. "Maybe we should put up our own basket."

"She's sure-enough good at it," Daddy mused.

An hour later I dragged myself into Sunday school. Just like the week before, everybody stared at me, and Kayla and her friends huddled closer together. A smothered burst of giggles escaped them, and I wondered if they were giggling about me. Shakara said hi to me, and I said hi back, but then she kept talking to Samantha.

I went straight into the classroom, even though it wasn't quite time, and sat down at the table. There was a Bible at each place, and the one in front of me was maroon with gold edges on the pages. I didn't touch it.

After a minute Ricky Talmadge bounced in, just ahead of the others. "Hi, Scissors," he grinned, sliding into a chair across from me. There was nothing mean about the way he said it, and I managed a faint little grin in response.

Mrs. Oakes's lesson was about how Jesus cared for bad people as much as good people, and how He was glad to eat and talk with anyone, even the most notorious sinners.

I didn't hear Jesus talking to me. But if He'd wanted to, He wouldn't have had much competition.

After lunch Daddy went to Kmart and came back with a backboard, hoop, net, and a pole in three sections, along with a hollow base and a bag of sand to fill it. Monica helped him take the things out of the station wagon and set them at the end of the driveway. I sat on the front step, between the two white concrete boxes full of geraniums, and watched.

It didn't take them long to set it up. Monica held the rim straight while Daddy screwed it onto the backboard, which was painted like an American flag, and she put on the red, white, and blue net while Daddy filled the base with sand. She was smiling and bouncing around like a kid on a pogo stick, in the very cool new basketball shoes Mama had bought her, in front of the new basket that Daddy was putting up just for her.

I couldn't remember ever seeing Daddy put something together. He wasn't the kind of dad who fixed leaky faucets or built a swing set or helped you with LEGO projects. He was the kind of dad who worked in a store all day and played golf on his days off. One thing for sure, he'd never done anything like this for me.

"You put it up crooked," I called from my perch on the step as soon as the basket was up.

They stepped back to look at it. "It's not crooked," Monica said.

"It is, too. It leans to the left."

Daddy folded his arms and narrowed his eyes at the basket. "It's about half a degree off. Which is pretty durn close to perfectly straight."

"Doesn't look straight to me," I said.

"Maybe your head's on crooked," said Daddy, and Monica laughed.

"Yeah, right," I answered furiously. "And that flag looks so dumb. That's the dumbest-looking hoop I ever saw," I threw over my shoulder as I went in the house and banged the screen door behind me.

I was dying of boredom, or something. I was sick of our house but there was nowhere to go. I didn't make phone calls, and no one called me. I read long books and made long lanyards and strung beads in long, boring necklaces. I sat by a window in the living room and stared out. I sat in the swing on the front porch, barely pushing off with my toes, just enough to move myself slowly back and forth, just enough to make the swing slowly, faintly squeak.

One afternoon, when I was sitting on my bed, staring down at the bag of beads I had just dropped, spilling most of them, the doorbell rang. I leaped up to answer it, hoping for I don't know what.

Russell Lovinger stood there on the front step. "Hey," he said. "Your sister home?"

"Yeah."

"Ask her if she wants to play some hoops, okay? We need one more player."

"Sure," I said, wishing it was me he was looking for. "Monica!"

In a minute she was out on the Lovingers' driveway, teaming up with Russell against two of his high-school friends. With nothing else to do, I dragged myself out to sit under a tree to watch. "Brucie!" I called, and he came trotting up to hang out with me.

"Hey, Russ," one of the other boys, named Josh something, said. "How 'bout we spot you ten points, since you got a girl on your team? We'll kick your butt anyway."

"You can spot us zippo," Russell answered. "And you ain't kicking nobody's butt."

"Woooo," grinned Josh's partner, without looking at anyone. He was trying to spin the basketball on his fingertip. "You better show us, tough guy."

"Bring it on," Monica piped up. The boys laughed, and she looked embarrassed. But once the game started, they stopped laughing. Monica's shooting put her and Russell way ahead in no time.

I watched a little, picked the leaves off clover, rubbed Bruce's belly, tried to whistle through grass blades. Every time Russell hollered out the score, he and Monica were further ahead.

But the really amazing thing happened *after* the game. Monica, who didn't have a friend in the world and never invited anybody over, actually asked the boys to come in for something to drink. And they actually said yes, and the four of them sat around the living room with lemonade and orange juice.

I poked around in the kitchen, listening. Maybe I'd make brownies. I found a mix, a measuring cup, eggs, a bottle of vegetable oil.

"You go to Marsh, don't you?" Josh said. "You play on their team?"

"No," said Monica.

"How come?"

"I don't know. I just never tried out."

"Well, you ought to. I bet they don't have a single girl plays as good as you."

"Yeah," said Russell. "You could probably play first string on the high-school team right now."

I stretched up to get a pan out of one of the cabinets, then peeked into the living room. Monica's face was flushed and happy. She was sitting right where she'd sat that Saturday when she opened her big mouth and told Mama I'd gone out in the night.

I cracked the egg too hard against the edge of the bowl and had to pick bits of shell out of the powdery, sweet-smelling mix.

Monica and the boys came in while I was stirring and put their glasses in the sink. Nobody spoke to me except Russell. "Mmmm, save me some brownies when you're done, okay?" He patted me on the head like I was a tiny little girl, and then they all bounced out of the house.

Once, just once, I got an e-mail from Hannah. She wrote me from San Francisco, using her mom's laptop. The subject line said *for Erin* because the address I'd given her was really Mama's, although Monica and I were allowed to use it now and then. I hardly ever got e-mail messages, so when Mama told me I had one, I knew it had to be from Hannah.

I ran over to the computer. "Did you read it?" I asked Mama.

"I don't read other people's mail." She got up so I could sit in front of the computer. "Don't be on a long time."

Dear Erin, Hannah had typed, on the other side of the country. *We are having a great trip except Jake and Laura are being annoying. You know how they are. I liked Disneyland the best. Yesterday we went to Chinatown and rode on a cable car. Everything is really crowded here. How are you? Are you going swimming a lot? We'll be home on August 10. Love, Hannah.*

August 10. I looked at the calendar that hung on the wall above the computer. I wouldn't even be here—I was going to church camp for a week on August 8. On the square for August 30 there were big red letters that Mama had printed: SCHOOL STARTS.

I read Hannah's letter again. She probably didn't know I'd been caught. She probably didn't want to even hint at anything about our adventure because she knew Mama or someone else might read her message. We had agreed not to mention anything secret on e-mail. But still, I wished there had been just the tiniest hint. I wished she had sounded like she was thinking about me. Somehow the message made me feel lonelier than ever.

I closed up e-mail and disconnected, then wandered into the kitchen, where Mama was wiping off the counters. "So that was from Hannah?" Mama asked. "Is she having a good trip?"

"Yeah, I guess so," I said, opening the refrigerator. I

didn't really want anything, and let it close itself. "They went to Disneyland. Now they're in San Francisco."

"Sounds nice."

I went to Mama and put my arms around her. I thought I might cry if I tried to say anything, and I didn't want to cry. She hugged me back. "I know you're bored," she said. "But you need some settling-down time, even if it's boring. And it won't be long till camp. Just five days."

The way I felt, five days might as well have been forever.

Chapter 17

Gilead

The week at Gilead Baptist Camp had been planned for months, but when the time finally came, I felt like I was being sent to reform school. Mr. Morton had finally assured Daddy that there would be no lawsuit, and that was a big relief. But just the same, I had a feeling my parents had been counting the days as much as I had, eager to get rid of me and the cloud of trouble I'd brought.

I'd spent a week at Gilead in each of the last two summers. I liked going on hikes, finding quartz crystals, singing in the dining hall after supper, swimming in the lake, just being in the mountains. It was a lot more camp than church, even though we did have a Bible reading in our cabins at bedtime and a service on Sunday morning.

Most of the kids were pretty cool, just normal kids, except sometimes you'd get one who was super-religious and wanted extra Bible studies, or told you, if you got mad about something, to think of what Jesus would do. And every year there was at least one preacher's kid in my group. They always swore a lot and told dirty jokes, and at breakfast they threw scrambled eggs at people.

The day we drove to camp was about the hottest day of the summer. It was Sunday, and we'd gone to church as usual. As soon as we got home I threw off my dress, slipped into shorts and a tank top, and checked the contents of my backpack and duffel bag one last time. After lunch, as soon as the dishes were in the dishwasher, all four of us piled into the car.

The air-conditioning in our old station wagon just barely worked, and the little bit of cool air it put out stayed in the front, where Mama and Daddy sat. It was so bad they finally turned it off and opened all the windows.

Monica sat beside me in the backseat, both of us sweating, with a backpack in the middle as a divider. I read a book most of the way. Monica said she'd get carsick if she read, so she took off her glasses—she had just gotten them the week before—and stared out the window with her Walkman on, fiddling with radio stations.

I was a lot more excited about camp than Monica was. She'd been complaining about going because there weren't any basketball hoops at Gilead. It was a nature camp—lots of hiking and canoeing but no regular sports.

I already knew that Monica and I wouldn't be in the same group, and I'd decided not to tell anyone that I had a sister at camp.

We shot through Asheville on the interstate, and I recognized road names on the exit signs and remembered our old house at the edge of the woods. I felt suddenly homesick for the exact shade of green that the back porch was painted, and for the smell of sassafras and the look of white and red trillium deep in the woods in spring.

Mama was homesick too. I could hear it in her voice when she said, "Look, girls, there's Carver Road. We'd go that way if we were going to our old house."

Finally, past Asheville and off the interstate, the road started climbing and the air got a little cooler. We were on a narrow, winding highway now, and I closed my book. I couldn't read with the car swaying heavily around the tight curves, and anyway I liked looking at the trees and steep hillsides with cows and sheep, and the tiny towns with just a gas station and a Tastee Freeze and maybe a Piggly Wiggly market.

Then we turned off on a smaller road, and then a slow, dusty gravel road lined with pine trees, and then around a curve and into the camp's gravel parking lot. It was full of vans and SUVs and station wagons, and kids running around, and piles of backpacks and sleeping bags. Counselors with name tags stuck to camp T-shirts were walking around with clipboards, checking off the new arrivals and pointing them toward cabins. A few parents and grand-parents sat in rockers on the dining-hall porch, fanning themselves with maps or magazines.

I got out first, slamming the car door behind me. Right away I spotted this really gross boy named Tommy who was in my group last year. He was a skinny kid who was always catching daddy longlegs and pulling their legs off, or making fart noises that sounded like the real thing. Half the time they probably *were* the real thing. He carried around a brown medicine bottle that he said contained essence of fart, and he'd open it up and wave it around after he made the noise. Sometimes you could smell it and sometimes you couldn't.

Next to the car, Mama and Daddy were talking to a counselor, and Monica was taking her backpack and sleeping bag out of the back. She wore a baggy old white T-shirt with a red cross on it that she'd gotten the summer before, when she helped give swimming lessons to little kids. And now she was wearing the new glasses, which were too big and made her look like a barn owl.

Daddy helped me carry my stuff to cabin five. The girls' side was empty—just three sets of metal bunk beds and a bare concrete floor—but two of the beds had sleeping bags and backpacks on them. We put my things on one of the top bunks and started out, just in time to see Tommy heading into the boys' side.

"Hiya," he said with a big grin.

"Hi," I muttered. I cruised right on out the door, but Daddy of course had to stop and chat with Tommy's mother, even though he'd never met her before. I scuffed around on the dirty path outside, all alone except for their voices and all the voices floating up from the parking lot, somewhere downhill and beyond the trees.

Mama came up the path, twisting her hair up in a pony-tail as she walked. "All set?" she said.

"Yeah, except Daddy's in there talking."

"That figures," she said, smiling. I wondered if she was happy to have me and Monica out of the house for a whole week. Probably she was especially happy to get rid of me.

"They still have those creaky metal beds," I complained. "And that really gross boy—remember the one I told you about last year?—he's in my group again."

"Well," said Mama, "maybe he's grown up a little by now." Which was pretty much exactly what I expected her to say.

"Oh yeah, right," I said.

She hated it when I was sarcastic. For a second she opened her mouth, then closed it firmly. "*Anyway*. Monica is all settled in cabin seven, and I told her the same thing I'm telling you: I want you two to look out for each other, all right?"

"Yeah, sure."

"You reckon you can do that?"

"I said yes, didn't I?"

"Erin Chaney, you do not speak to your mother in that tone of voice."

"Sorry," I muttered as Daddy came out of the cabin toward us.

Mama held my face in her hands. "Start fresh, Erin. It's going to be fine. *You're* fine."

We walked down the path to the dining-hall porch, where my counselors were waiting with a few kids next to a sign that said CABIN 5 — BOBCATS.

"Bye, punkin," Daddy said, and they both hugged me, and then they got in the car and drove away.

"Erin, come on over," the girl counselor called. "I'm Amy." She had shoulder-length blond hair and an open, cheerful face. On her camp T-shirt was a rainbow pin, with little gold letters under the rainbow that said SMILE, GOD LOVES YOU.

Isabel sat cross-legged on the top bunk across from mine, her head almost touching the ceiling. She was a pale girl with wide blue eyes that always looked slightly surprised. She was from Asheville, so I'd told her right away that I used to live there, but she lived in a different part of town and went to a school I didn't remember.

It was quiet time after lunch. We had to stay in our bunks, but we could read or draw or write, or even talk if we kept our voices down. In the other room, one of the boys was groaning, "Why don't they let us have Game Boys?"

"Do you have any brothers and sisters?" Isabel wanted to know, fiddling with one of her long, light brown braids.

"Yeah," I said. "I have a sister. Do you have any?"

"Oh boy, do I have brothers and sisters. Three little brats that drive me crazy. Robbie is eight—he's in cabin three—and Angela and Andrea are five. They're twins."

"Wow. It must be cool to be a twin," I said.

"Well, it's not cool to have twin little sisters, believe me," Isabel answered. "Everybody thinks they're sooo cute. Most of the time they're a pain in the butt. At least they're too little to come to camp." She drummed her fingers on the railing of the bed. "How old is your sister?"

"Almost fourteen."

"Is she pretty?"

Yeah, right, I thought. "Oh . . . she's okay," I said.

"Is she at camp?"

I shook my head and said quickly, "Hang on, I've gotta go to the bathroom." I scrambled down from the bunk, giving Isabel one quick glance before heading for the door. She looked a little surprised at my abrupt exit. Or maybe that was just the way her big blue eyes always looked.

We got our meals in the camp dining hall, which had a concrete floor and a high roof with no ceiling, just open rafters. We sat on benches at long tables and passed around heavy white bowls and platters, helping ourselves to spaghetti or beans or corn bread or biscuits. When we were finished eating, we had to take our plates to a table near the kitchen and scrape the leftover bits into a revolting bucket.

Every year at the first meal, the camp director, Reverend Mr. Haywood, told us we had to do this; instead of wasting the leftovers, we saved them for a farmer who would pick them up to feed his pigs. Sometimes Mr. Haywood watched, and if you didn't scrape your plate thoroughly, he'd say, "Mr. Johnson's pigs are going to be mighty hungry tonight if you don't do better than that. Give 'em another bite or two." You'd have to scrape it again, and you'd be embarrassed, too, because Mr. Haywood had a voice like a church organ, and the whole room would hear him telling you to scrape.

After supper—after the tables were cleared and wiped off with sponges—we sat around singing for a while, led by Mr. Haywood. Our "songbooks" were just sheets of paper stapled together, but a lot of us didn't need them anyway. There were strange old songs with haunting words:

I'll sing you two ho
Green grow the rushes ho
What is your two ho?
Two, two, the lily-white boys
Clothéd all in green ho
One is one and all alone
and ever more shall be so.

And there were hymns, rousing ones like "Onward Christian Soldiers" and sweet ones like "Shall We Gather at the River." There were silly songs, too, and rounds, and folk songs.

Three tables over, I could see Monica singing with her group. I was glad I wasn't sitting next to her; she sang like a bullfrog. And I was glad no one here knew that she was my sister.

Since this was Gilead Baptist Camp, the singing always ended with "There Is a Balm in Gilead." Tommy and a few others sang a different version, very quietly in the dining hall and louder as we walked back to our cabins:

> *There is a bomb in Gilead*
> *To blast a great big hole;*
> *There is a bomb in Gilead*
> *Let's blow the camp to hell.*

The lake was cold, and water lilies spread their big floating leaves across part of it, not far from the sandy beach where we waded in. The water was dark—not muddy or dirty, but clear dark in a way that made me think of iron and minerals and mountain streams. It tasted of rock and metal, like drinking from a tin cup.

It was the afternoon of the third day of camp, and my group was going swimming. We all took off our shoes and dropped our towels on the beach, then headed for the water. Tommy and a boy named Kevin ran straight in, yelling, and flopped spread-eagled, smacking the surface. The other boy, Rashad, wasn't far behind. Isabel waded in, then dived and came up, shaking back a waterfall of hair and gasping.

A plump girl named Zoe and I were the slowest, shivering as each step encircled a few more inches of leg in cold water. "Good Lord," Zoe said. "This is like an ice-water bath."

"Just dive in," said Jeff, the boy counselor. "It's a lot less painful." He waded out to the depth of his knees, then dived and swam with long, slow strokes out to the dock, where Amy had already climbed out and lay dripping in the sun.

I watched as Jeff's head appeared beside the dock, and he hung on to the ladder, talking to Amy. Isabel had told me she'd seen them kissing outside the cabin last night when she got up to pee. I studied them as I stood thigh-deep in the lake, hugging myself, wanting to see if they looked at each other in a special way. Jeff was cute, with big shoulders and hands, and long legs, and kind of a sweet smile. When I thought of him and Amy kissing I felt warm, deep inside, and fascinated. I wished I had seen them.

Isabel had told me about it on the way to breakfast, and she told me not to tell anyone else. "You're the only one I'm telling," she said. "Zoe and Tina are a little bit immature. I'm sure Amy wouldn't want them to know. I don't think they'd understand about being in love."

"Yeah," I agreed quickly, flattered. "They're both kind of immature."

We sat down side by side on a bench at one of the long tables in the dining hall, along with the rest of our group.

"Hey." I'd suddenly thought of something. "Do they know you saw them?" I whispered to Isabel.

"I don't think so." She gave me a cunning smile. "They were kind of . . . busy."

I smiled the same smile back, and then we had to stop talking because Reverend Haywood boomed out, "This is the day the Lord hath made. Let's give Him thanks."

At the lake I saw Isabel watching Jeff and Amy, too, but soon, since there wasn't anything special to see, we just swam. After the first plunge and shriek it was fine. I did a backstroke out toward the dock, looking up at hot blue sky with my mouth and nose just out of the water.

Mama was right, I thought—camp *was* a fresh start. Jeff and Amy were nice, I liked hanging around with Isabel, and everyone else was at least okay. Even Tommy hadn't been as gross as I remembered; he hadn't even brought the essence of fart. In the three days we'd been here, I'd hardly seen Monica, except in the crowded dining hall, several tables away, and no one knew I had a sister at camp. I'd almost forgotten about Kayla's hair, about being grounded and lonely, about faraway Hannah, my best friend.

I felt like a new person. Or maybe like the person I used to be, before this summer.

Right then I squirmed around to see if I was about to bump into the dock. I wasn't, but something else was almost on top of me—a canoe, and Monica was in it. "Hey there," she said.

"You almost ran over me," I spluttered, treading water.

"Sorry, didn't see you," called the girl in the stern.

"Oh, I wouldn't run over my own sister," said Monica, blinking owlishly behind her big glasses, and dipped her paddle. The canoe glided by, toward the shore where other canoes in the group were already landing. Each one had GILEAD BAPTIST CAMP stenciled on the side in white letters.

Stupid Monica, I thought. The feeling of starting fresh had vanished. I turned toward the dock, and there was Amy, dangling her feet over the edge. "Erin, that's your sister?" she said. "I didn't know you had a sister here."

"Oh," I said. "Yeah."

"You look a little bit like her," remarked Amy cheerfully.

"I don't think so," I said, and ducked under the surface. I swam underwater all the way around to the other side of the dock.

Hanging on to the rough boards, I watched as Monica's group pulled the canoes up on the beach and took off life jackets. A couple of the boys were splashing each other in the shallows, smacking the water with paddles, until a counselor told them to cut it out. The four other girls in the group were paired off, talking and laughing as they waded into the lake. Only Monica stood by herself, still holding the orange life jacket and looking around, as if she'd landed in a foreign country and didn't know what she was supposed to do there.

Chapter 18

Fire Starting

Every week at Gilead, there was a campout on Friday night. I liked camping, and one of the good things about it this year was that I wouldn't catch even a glimpse of Monica, whose group would be camping at a different site, miles away.

My group hiked about five miles from Gilead, to a campsite called Crow's Nest, on a hilltop in a state forest. Hot and tired, we dropped our heavy backpacks in the clearing and looked around. It was about six in the evening, and we still had a lot to do if we were going to cook dinner over an open fire and sleep in tents that night.

Right away, Amy and Jeff sent every last one of us out to

gather firewood. The woods were still slightly damp from the hard rain two nights ago, and it wasn't easy to find dry tinder and kindling.

When most of us had come back with an armload, Jeff told me to fetch a bucket of water from the creek at the bottom of the hill, and assigned other kids to start on the tents and the fire.

I went off swinging my bucket. It wasn't far to the creek, but here in the state forest the woods were dense, much thicker than the woods around Gilead. I hadn't gotten ten feet beyond the edge of the clearing before I felt, with a shiver that was part pleasure and part fear, that I was alone in deep wilderness.

The path down to the creek was rough, studded with rocks and tree roots. Little carpets of moss, soft as velvet, grew beside the path, nestled around the base of the trees. There were huge oaks and maples, and tiny baby ones underneath, leggy and starving for light. Mountain laurel and rhododendron grew everywhere in thickets.

To shake off that slight nervousness about being alone here, I tried to think of these woods as Lothlorien, the magical forest of the elves, where the good and powerful spirits of Galadriel and Celeborn ruled. I was Frodo, small beneath the trees but safe, so perfectly safe. I had been permitted, because of my all-important quest, to take refuge in this magnificent forest that few besides elves were ever allowed to enter.

The mountain laurel, though, kept getting in the way of my dreamy thoughts. Something had happened four years ago, and I still couldn't see a laurel thicket without remembering.

I was seven, and Monica told me she'd read in the newspaper about a seven-year-old boy being lost in the mountains. He'd gone off playing in the woods while his family had a picnic in some little roadside park. The article said the mountain laurel was so dense and mazelike around there, and the laurel thickets were so vast, that even a grown-up could easily get lost. Those thickets, the worst ones, were called laurel hells by mountain people.

I had never heard the term *laurel hells* until Monica read this to me, and it sounded horrible; it haunted me. A familiar big green bush, with clusters of pretty flowers, turned into something monstrous, something a child my age could disappear into and never come back. And that boy was never found. For days the newspapers were full of stories about the search—I'd begun reading the paper myself, despite all the hard words—but the stories got shorter and shorter, and finally vanished altogether.

I had nightmares about being trapped in a laurel hell, stems twining around my wrists, branches tripping my feet. Faraway voices were calling me anxiously, but I couldn't raise my own voice above a hoarse whisper, and no one could find me.

I shuddered, remembering those nightmares, but managed to put them out of my mind. There was still plenty of daylight left. The path was plain and I would not leave it. I could hear the creek splashing, not far ahead.

When I got back to the clearing and set down the heavy bucket, Zoe was dragging herself in from the opposite side, holding a few sticks. Everyone else was working on tents or food or the fire. It figured that Zoe would be the last one back. We'd been on three hikes, counting the trek out here, and every time she lagged behind the group. Kevin started calling her "Zoe Slowy."

I stood precariously on a boulder, arms out for balance, watching the three boys hovering around the sputtering little fire they'd just managed to start.

"No, man, that's no good. Leaves'll just smoke up the place," Kevin was saying. "Don't you know better?"

"Ah, I was just fooling around," said Rashad. He was a small boy, a head shorter than the others, with skin like dark chocolate. "I wasn't going to put them in the fire." For a second he looked down at a handful of last year's oak leaves. Suddenly he tossed them up in the air, and they came whirling down all over the place.

"City boy," Kevin grinned, poking a twig into the tiny flames.

Rashad *was* about to put those leaves on the fire, I was sure. He lived in the middle of Charlotte, and this was the first time he'd ever been to camp.

Nearby, Isabel and Tina had finished setting up one of the two girls' tents, but they were still struggling with the other one. On the far side of the clearing, the boys' tents were already standing, though one sagged in the middle and the other leaned to one side.

The flames, gnawing at twigs under a tepee of small branches, seemed to be faltering. Tommy was on his knees, blowing on them.

"Hey!" Kevin said. "You're just gonna blow it out."

"No, I'm not. Fire needs oxygen. I'm giving it some extra oxygen."

"Put some of this on," said Kevin, prodding Tommy's back with a handful of twigs. "Come on, try some of this."

Tommy ignored him and sat back on his heels. "It's this tepee thing," he pronounced. "You guys made it with too-big branches."

"No, we didn't," Kevin said. "You're full of—"

"Just in time, Kevin," called Amy. "You stopped yourself just in time."

"Tell you what," Jeff said, walking over to the boys. "How about Amy and I help you guys out a little? We'll scout around and see if we can find some really dry stuff, something that'll burn better than this."

Isabel elbowed my side. When Amy and Jeff walked off, down a path into the woods, she raised her eyebrows and whispered. "Off to be alone together."

"Tweet tweet tweet," Tommy chirped. "There go the lovebirds."

Isabel and I stared at him.

"Sure," he said, seeing our faces. "Didn't you know about them? Kissy kissy all the time."

"Well, of course *we* knew," Isabel said haughtily. "But we weren't going to blab about it."

"Is that really true?" said Zoe. "Are they—?"

By now the whole group was standing around the fire, listening.

It was totally annoying to have our secret, mine and Isabel's, revealed to the entire world. Especially since it was a grown-up kind of secret, a secret about adult lives, about romance. "Tommy, you are so gross," I said. "Why do you have to go blabbing?"

Most of the kids were grinning. Kevin was pretending to throw up.

Tommy ignored me. "Let's go spy on them," he said, looking at the other boys.

"Naah," Kevin said. "I'm in charge of the fire."

Rashad just shook his head.

Tommy shrugged. "Farewell, then." With knee-high, tiptoeing steps, like a cartoon villain, he crossed the clearing and disappeared down the narrow path.

Everybody watched him go.

"That's mean," said Tina. She was a small, thin girl with a chirpy little voice. Kevin called her Tiny Tina.

"He's awful," said Zoe.

"Extremely immature," was Isabel's comment.

"Why do boys have to act like idiots?" I complained.

"Because they *are* idiots," Tina answered, at exactly the same time that Isabel said, "Because they're boys."

All four of the girls laughed.

Rashad said, "Ah, y'all are just dumb girls. You probably like that yucky stuff. I bet you go on the Internet and find pictures. Sex dot-com."

"You're just plain nasty," Zoe accused, wrinkling her nose.

"Ignore him, Zoe," advised Isabel in her loftiest tone. "Remarks like that don't deserve an answer."

Some balance of power had shifted, now that there were twice as many girls as boys. Isabel seemed to feel it too, because instead of walking away, she folded her arms and stared disapprovingly at Rashad. He just grinned back, then sat down on a big log near the fire, watching Kevin take random pokes at it with a long stick.

"Can't count on lovebirds to bring back any fuel," Kevin said, to no one in particular. "If they find any dry twigs, they'll just make themselves a nest."

At that moment the fire sputtered out completely.

A look of outraged disbelief spread over Kevin's freckled face. "We had it going. It was starting to catch. Then it just went and died. Stupid thing." He kicked the blackened tepee sticks halfway across the clearing.

"Oops, you did it again," Isabel sang softly into an imaginary microphone. "You messed up your fie-yer. Oops, you did it again."

Tina and Zoe and I giggled.

"Shut. Up." With an exasperated sigh Kevin stared around the area, then spoke to Rashad. "What it needs is something that'll really burn fast. We got any more pine needles?"

Rashad, still sitting on the log, pointed to a branch lying nearby. "Right there."

Kevin rolled his eyes. "Those are green, smart one."

Rashad flinched. "Well, you're so smart, how come there's no dinner cooking?"

Kevin reddened, twisting a stick in his hands. It was too green to break. "Least I know better than to put a bunch of old leaves on the fire. Right, raisin?"

Rashad stood up, his hands in fists. "What you call me?"

This was trouble. I looked around for Amy and Jeff, but they hadn't returned, and neither had Tommy. The other girls, alerted by Rashad's tone, stopped talking and watched.

"Nothing, nothing, man," Kevin protested, giving the smaller boy a friendly punch to the shoulder. At least I guess it was friendly. I never understood why boys whacked each other all the time.

Tossing the stick aside, Kevin raised both hands. "Just kidding around. Don't take it personal." But he didn't sound apologetic. More like annoyed.

Rashad just glared. "What do you mean, calling me raisin?" he demanded.

"Well," Kevin shrugged, "you're little and you're black. Like a raisin. Okay, raisin?"

He started to turn away, but then in one unbelievably quick motion Rashad crouched, grabbed a rock, and hurled it. It caught Kevin on the side of the head and he staggered for a second, then gave a strange little yelp and stood still. Another second and blood was matting his hair. Slowly he raised a hand to his head, brought it down, and stared at the red that covered it.

The rest of us stood paralyzed until he began to cry and curse Rashad, his whole body shaking.

"Oh my gosh, oh my gosh," Tina kept saying.

"Where's the first-aid kit?" cried Zoe in a frightened voice. She looked wildly around, and so did Isabel and I. It was nowhere in sight. Kevin sank down and sat on the ground, sobbing.

"It must be in Amy's pack, or Jeff's," I said, and ran over to a heap of backpacks. My heart was pounding so hard, my chest hurt.

"I'm going to find them!" Tina cried, and ran off down the path Amy and Jeff had taken, and Tommy too, what seemed like a long time ago. Before she was out of sight, she was yelling, "Amy! Jeff!" Her voice drifted away on the breeze that had sprung up, rustling the trees. She kept calling every few seconds, but the calls became faint and fainter, and died away.

The counselors' packs were easy to spot because they were so much bigger than the ones the kids carried. I rummaged through Amy's, scattering some of her things on the ground. Flashlight, sweatshirt, lotion, underwear. No kit. I finally found it in Jeff's pack, a white plastic box with a red cross on top.

When I stood, holding up the kit, relieved that I'd done something at least, I took in the scene: Zoe and Isabel bending over Kevin, the scattered sticks of the failed campfire at their feet, the green backdrop of trees behind them. Nothing and nobody else. Rashad was gone.

Chapter 19

Injuries

I ran over with the first-aid kit and Isabel reached for it. "I'll do it," she said. "I took a first-aid course at school."

That was fine with me. I couldn't look at Kevin's head or his bloodied hand without feeling sick.

"I'll do it myself," Kevin muttered. He had stopped crying and was looking up now, though not exactly looking any of us in the eye. I guessed he was embarrassed because he'd been crying so much, and maybe because of all the attention from Zoe and Isabel and me.

But Isabel wasn't handing over the box. "You can't see the side of your own head, Kevin," she said in a reasonable, motherly tone. "Now just hold still."

She took out a piece of gauze and told Zoe to dip it in one of the water buckets and bring it back. She washed the blood off Kevin's head, dabbed some ointment on it, and put a big chunk of gauze on the wound, taping it down. It didn't stick very well because it had to be taped partly across Kevin's hair.

Once that was done, Kevin's head didn't look so bad, and I felt some of the tightness in my stomach relax a little. "Is it still bleeding?" I asked.

"Not much," Isabel answered briskly, putting the tape and scissors and gauze and ointment neatly back into the kit.

"You should be a nurse someday," Zoe said admiringly.

"I think I'll be a brain surgeon," Isabel said.

Kevin stood up slowly and moved away from us, muttering, "I'm okay now." We silently watched him get a cup out of his backpack, dip it into the water bucket, and drink.

Then I remembered. "Where'd Rashad go?" Isabel and Zoe looked blankly back at me. Kevin, sitting on a rock next to the bucket, looked around and said some really bad words about Rashad.

"I don't know," Zoe said. "He was standing right there a minute ago."

"Who cares? I hope he stays gone," said Isabel. "He threw a rock at Kevin's *head*." She looked over at her patient and nodded, seeming to approve of his progress.

"He's an animal," Zoe agreed.

"Well," I said, "Kevin did call him a name."

"It wasn't that bad a name," said Isabel. "Anyway, that doesn't give him the right to throw a rock at somebody."

"Yeah," said Zoe. She lowered her voice. "He's one of those inner-city black kids. They fight all the time. Rocks and knives and baseball bats."

I didn't know why I was defending Rashad—I'd been horrified by the rock and the blood, and I didn't even like him very much—but I heard my voice rising as I stared at Zoe. "How do you know he's like that? He never acted like that before. And Kevin was really mean to him. Kevin called him raisin, and made fun of him for not knowing about fires."

"Maybe," Zoe said meekly, not meeting my eyes. She turned away and began gathering up some of the scattered sticks. I could tell she wasn't convinced—she just didn't want to argue.

Isabel was giving me a strange look, as though I'd said something really weird. But all she said was, "Why is it taking so long for everybody else to get back?"

At that moment Tina came hurrying into the clearing, with Amy and Jeff right behind her. Amy looked anxious, but relief crossed her face as soon as she saw Kevin sitting up, with a bandage on, looking basically okay. She and Jeff knelt beside him, asking him questions and examining the wound.

Jeff looked around. "Who's got the first-aid kit?"

Isabel brought it to him, but as she handed it over she

said, "I cleaned it and put antibiotic on it. You don't need to do anything to it."

"Izzy, you done good," he said, and he smiled in a way that made my heart flip, and Isabel's, too, because I could see her melt. He was so good-looking, and he had that easy, grown-up authority, even though he was probably just six or seven years older than us. For a second I imagined being a mature sixteen, and meeting him again somewhere. He would have broken up with Amy long ago, and he'd be lonely; he wouldn't recognize me as a kid from camp; he'd sit next to me and smile that way but only for me.

"Where did Rashad go?" Amy was standing with her hands on her hips, looking around the clearing.

"We don't know," Isabel answered. "He disappeared while we were taking care of Kevin."

The worried frown was back on Amy's face, the blond eyebrows pulled together.

"Should we go look for him?" I said. "We could each take a different path."

There were four paths leading out of the clearing—the one we had come in on, which passed through several miles of woods to a road that led to Gilead; the one down to the creek; and two others that I knew nothing about beyond the first twenty feet.

"No," said Jeff. "Everybody's staying right here. We don't need you guys wandering around the woods getting lost."

"But what if Rashad's lost?" I said. I thought of the laurel hells and there was a cold knot in my stomach. Rashad was smaller than any of us, small enough to duck under laurel branches, going deeper and deeper into the maze.

"He's probably pretty upset and just needs some time to be alone," Amy said. "He'll come back when he's ready." But I saw her look over at Jeff, as if hoping he would confirm her words, and I realized then that she wasn't as sure as she sounded.

Night was coming down, midnight blue through the tops of the trees. We could hear cicadas and crickets, and occasionally an unexplained rustle or crackle from somewhere out in the woods, but nobody said a word, not after Amy ended the time of silent prayer with a quiet "amen," and some of us murmured "amen" in response.

We were sitting on logs and stones around the fire. Tommy, coached by Jeff, had managed to get it going, even though the counselors had come back from the woods empty-handed. And it took a long time, but finally we'd boiled hot dogs and heated some baked beans, and after we ate we'd toasted marshmallows and gobbled s'mores until the marshmallows and chocolate were gone.

We were all there. Rashad had slipped back into the midst of us during the cooking, well before dark, and he hadn't answered when Tina said, "Where were you? Did you get lost?" Kevin gave him dirty looks and Zoe quit stirring the beans, letting the spoon fall into the pot as she stared.

I didn't say anything, but a wave of relief washed over me, sweeping away the thoughts of laurel hells, and lostness, and the gathering dark.

Jeff had stepped over to Rashad, saying, "Give him a break, everybody—back to your jobs." He put an arm around Rashad's shoulders and steered him away from the group. "You doing okay?" I heard as they walked away. They talked for a minute, and then Jeff called Kevin over. That discussion took longer, but it ended in a handshake between the two boys. From where I stood, setting out the plates and cups on a stump near the fire, it looked like both of them were pretty reluctant.

We all cooked and ate and cleaned up and talked without even mentioning the fight. And after the s'mores, with everybody settled around the fire, Amy said, in a voice that carried over the chatter, "There's something I want to say to all of you."

No cheerleader smile now. She looked seriously into each of our faces, and we got quiet.

"Jeff and I made a mistake," she said quietly, "leaving you kids here for a while without an adult. That wasn't good thinking on our part."

She paused as if to let us think about that, and then she continued. "Kevin made a mistake in being unkind to Rashad. Rashad made a mistake in reacting violently. And I believe some of the rest of us made mistakes, too. I wasn't here to see what led up to this incident, but I'm pretty sure there were opportunities for other people to help Kevin and Rashad feel better instead of feeling so angry. And maybe some of us even added to the angry feelings. These boys were having some frustration, some dispute, because the fire was so hard to start, and maybe some of us were teasing them instead of helping.

"Let's have a silent prayer now, and ask God to forgive us for our mistakes—the things we did, and the things we didn't do but should have. And if we all do that, I promise you, tomorrow will be a better day."

For a few long minutes I heard nothing but the fire softly popping and hissing, cicadas buzzing, leaves sighing in the breeze. Words formed in my head. Things I should have done. I could have helped, maybe, before things got so bad between Kevin and Rashad. Things I shouldn't have done, but did, far from these green mountains.

Slowly, after the soft *amen*s, we all began to stir, some heading off toward the tents, or maybe into the woods to pee. I lingered, sitting by the fire, poking at the red coals with a stick to see the sparks fly.

As I bent toward the fire I saw a pair of sneakers right next to me and looked up. Rashad was standing there. "I just wanted to say thanks for sticking up for me," he said, so quietly I could hardly hear him.

I was startled. "What do you mean?"

"I was sitting over there in the bushes the whole time. I heard those other girls say I was an animal, stuff like that, and you said I had a reason, 'cause Kevin was such a jerk, calling me names, and, you know . . ." He trailed off, then said firmly, "So thanks."

"Oh. That's okay." I hesitated and then, with a strange sense of daring, added, "I got back at somebody who was mean to me, too. I really got her back."

"What did you do to her?"

"Cut off her hair."

"Whoa," Rashad said. He sat down on the nearest log. "How'd you do that? I mean, was she sitting still for it?"

"She was asleep. In a tent in her backyard."

"No joke," he said wonderingly.

I stared at the fire. Some of the coals still held the shape of the branches, the grain of the wood showing black through the red glow, and the whole thing brittle and about to collapse.

"Rashad," I said, "did throwing the rock make you feel better?"

"Sure. I paid that sucker back." But after a second he added, "I mean, I felt better for a minute, and then I felt worse."

I nodded. "Same with cutting her hair off."

"Yeah," Rashad said. "I guess so."

Chapter 20

Stuck

Sunday morning, the last day of camp. At least it was the last for Monica and me, though some of the other kids would be staying another week. My clothes were packed, my sleeping bag rolled up. Parents were coming between ten and twelve to pick everyone up. But first, after breakfast, there was a church service at the Sanctuary.

The Sanctuary was a clearing in the woods near the top of a hill, with rows of rough benches made of logs split in half. Mr. Haywood stood in front with his hands folded across his belly as we settled ourselves on the benches. He had keen blue eyes, and sometimes he seemed like a big jolly Santa Claus, but not now. "Quietly, please," he said sternly to some kids who were chattering as they entered the clearing. "This is the house of the Lord."

There wasn't enough room for all of us on the benches, so we had to squeeze together, and even then, some people had to stand in the back, among the trees. I was crammed between Isabel and Zoe. Squirming around to watch, I saw that Monica's group was the last to arrive. They spread out in the back, leaning against trees.

Mr. Haywood kept watching with his grave stare until everyone was quiet.

Then it really did seem like the house of the Lord, more than any church building I'd ever set foot in. Behind Mr. Haywood, at the top of the hill, there was a rough cross made out of two slender logs lashed together, and it made a dark silhouette against the eastern sky. The sun was streaming in through a screen of leaves, and a little breeze was blowing, and bright bits of sky jostled with the glowing green of leaves filtering the sun. Birds called in the trees all around us, blue jays and robins and mockingbirds.

We sang, "Morning has broken, like the first morning; blackbird has spoken, like the first bird," and the song seemed written for this place, and the day seemed new.

I didn't really listen to the Bible readings or the sermon. I watched the birds and the leaves, and brushed a daddy longlegs off the back of a kid in front of me. I was glad to be going home, glad that Mama and Daddy would soon be here.

I thought I was glad that Hannah would be back in

Shipley, too. I could hang out with her, since Mama had said I wouldn't be grounded after camp. Hannah was probably the only kid in my class who didn't think I was crazy, after what I'd done to Kayla.

And yet, other thoughts kept creeping in, making me uncertain of how I'd feel, seeing Hannah again. Cutting Kayla's hair had been Hannah's idea. She'd come up with the plan, scouted out the tents, put the scissors in my hands, urged me to do it. She'd done almost as much as I had—but *she* hadn't gotten caught. She'd been riding roller coasters at Disneyland and eating at fancy restaurants in San Francisco while I'd been grounded and disgraced.

But Hannah was my best friend. She'd stuck with me when Kayla and her pals had treated me like I was nothing. She'd wanted to hurt Kayla for *my* sake.

I shook my head as if that would somehow clear the muddle inside. All around me heads were bowed, and I quickly bent my head too, until Mr. Haywood said, "In the name of the Lord Jesus Christ, amen." Then, after a moment of silence, he smiled broadly, stretched out his arms toward us, and said, "Go in peace."

The service was over. People were standing up and stretching, starting to leave. Then Mr. Haywood's voice boomed out again. "Before you go, I'd like to have a word with Monica Chaney and Erin Chaney. Where are you, girls?"

I stiffened, wondering for a moment if I'd done something bad, but I knew I hadn't. What did he want with us?

"What's that about?" asked Isabel. "Are you in trouble?"

"I don't know," I said.

"Who's Monica Chaney? Is that your sister?"

But I pretended not to hear, and squeezed past her to the aisle, moving against the flow of everyone else, toward the pastor standing in front of the cross.

Monica and I sat in the dining hall, each on the end of a bench, at diagonally opposite corners of the same table. We were the only people in the room.

From outside, through the screen doors, we could hear a lot of people talking, a few good-bye shouts, repeated crunching of tires on gravel. Inside, there wasn't a sound except the buzzing of a few big flies.

Most of the kids were leaving camp. But we weren't.

I put my elbows on the table and stared down at it, twirling hair around my index finger. In third grade I was always doing that, and Mama was always after me to stop it. I finally did, but now, after all that time, it felt good. It felt like I *needed* some old bad habit to resurrect.

Monica was picking at a hangnail, then tracing a finger along the initials and hearts carved into the rough wood of the table.

One of the screen doors banged open. I looked around and saw Tina heading toward me. "There you are! Why aren't you out front with everybody else?"

"Oh—just—" As I stumbled over words I saw her glance curiously at Monica, then back at me, as if wondering how we were connected.

"What did Reverend Haywood say to you?" she demanded.

"Just—my parents are going to be late, that's all. I didn't want to hang around out there and watch everybody else leave."

"Oh," Tina said. "Well, listen, my folks are waiting for me—I have to go. But I just wanted to say bye. Maybe I'll see you next year, okay?"

"Sure," I said. "I come every summer." But even as I said it, I felt my certainty slipping away, and heard my voice getting smaller.

"Okay. Bye!" She dashed out, banging the door again. Someone was tapping a car horn over and over, whether out of impatience or as a good-bye, I couldn't tell.

What Mr. Haywood had told us, as we sat on one of the front benches in the Sanctuary, with him sitting on the end of the bench across the aisle, was that Daddy had called and asked if we could stay another week. Mama was going to have an operation, and he needed to be with her or at his job as much as possible. He didn't have time to look after us.

Neither of us said anything for a bit as we took this in. I felt as though a big space had opened up somewhere inside the top of my head and was pressing against my skull.

Mr. Haywood sat leaning toward us, arms resting on his thighs, hands clasped in front of his knees. I watched his big puffy fingers flexing slightly. He shifted his grasp, running a finger over his wedding ring again and again. For some reason I couldn't take my eyes off those fingers, as though they were not just parts of him but independent creatures, and I was some kind of naturalist intent on observing them.

Monica found her voice first. "What kind of operation?"

"Well," Mr. Haywood said, "it's an operation concerning the female organs. It's—well—" Now the hands unclasped, and my eyes followed one of them up to his chin, which he scratched for a moment. He sat up straighter now, and his broad face was calm, the sharp blue eyes moving from one to the other of us. I had a feeling he was used to giving people bad news.

"Your daddy will explain it all to you," he said finally. "He wants you to call him collect this afternoon, or this evening. He wasn't too sure when he'd be home."

"But," I started shakily, "is it—?"

"Serious?"

I nodded. This was the kind of question that grown-ups often wouldn't answer straight out—they'd give you part of the answer, or they'd say something soothing that didn't soothe you at all because you knew you weren't getting the whole story. So I watched Mr. Haywood closely as he answered.

"I don't know. Your daddy didn't tell me. But I know he's taking care of her, and some good doctors are too, so I reckon things will be all right." I looked hard, but his face didn't tell me any more than his words.

We sat in the dining hall a long time, listening to other kids leaving. I knew we weren't the only ones staying on for another week—Isabel was staying, and I was glad of that—but those kids had known all along. They were out running around, saying good-bye to other campers. Monica and I were too stunned for that.

Monica wandered over to the game table in the corner and came back with a deck of cards. I thought she was going to suggest a game of War or Go Fish, and I was going to say no. But instead she began laying out solitaire.

I watched the cards going *smack smack* against the table as she counted them out into neat piles. Nothing else moved in the whole huge room, except an occasional fly zooming past or landing briefly on the table. The noise from the parking lot was lessening, and I could hear clattering in the kitchen, where someone was making lunch.

A screen door creaked open and both of us looked up. It was a counselor I didn't know except by sight, and he gave us a curious glance but went straight to the kitchen.

Now it was my turn to wander to the game table. It was covered with battered old board games in boxes held together with masking tape: Monopoly, Clue, Life, Chinese checkers. There were more decks of cards, jigsaw puzzles, a wooden maze that you tilted to roll a metal ball to the finish. I shuffled halfheartedly through the games, finally settling on a puzzle with interlocking metal shapes.

I took the puzzle back to my seat, diagonally across the table from Monica and her solitaire. Though last year, after many tries, I'd finally solved this puzzle, now I couldn't remember how. The pieces jingled as I twisted and turned them every way I could think of, but the star refused to be untangled.

The screen door creaked again, and again Monica and I both looked up. This time it was Amy, and she came over and sat down next to me.

"So you're going to stick around, Erin!" she said cheerfully. She turned to Monica. "Hi. I'm Amy. It'll be nice to have you too, Monica."

"Hi," Monica said, with her eyes on the cards.

"Isabel's staying, right?" I asked.

"Right. And Jeff and I will still be your counselors, and Tommy and Kevin are staying too."

"Tommy and Kevin?" I made a face.

"What's wrong with them? I mean, besides being boys," she said teasingly.

"Oh, I don't know," I shrugged. I didn't feel like making any jokes about boys, and Amy's eternal cheeriness was irritating me.

"Which cabin will I be in?" Monica asked.

"Oh—I almost forgot. You'll be in cabin five with us."

"What?" I said, straightening up.

"I just talked to Mr. Haywood about it. The group for your age is totally full next week, Monica—no beds left in the cabin. And Erin's group was already small, and yesterday one of the girls called and canceled. So he decided you could join our group and be with your sister."

I felt panic rising in my throat. This was too much. Mama was having an operation, and I couldn't see her or Daddy for another week, or Hannah either. And now I was going to be stuck with Monica for the whole week. Now everybody would know this dork was my sister.

I stared at her—at her too-big glasses, her baggy shirt— and thought of how she'd blurted out the words that got me caught and grounded, the words that made Mama drag me to Kayla's door, to apologize and be humiliated. I wanted to have a screaming tantrum.

I held it in.

Then Monica met my eyes and flinched. She knew I didn't want her around, and realizing that made me feel so guilty, I wanted to kick her. My right leg twitched.

"I'm going outside," I said breathlessly, and ran. But as soon as the screen door banged behind me, out on the wide concrete porch, I stopped. Beyond the porch the midday sun made a wall of heat and glare. Harsh light ricocheted off the few remaining cars, a couple of signs, a million gravel stones flecked with mica.

Somehow that wall of glare told me there was nowhere to go. Slowly I walked to one end of the porch and sat on the edge of a rocking chair, where I kept very still and studied the floor. Gray concrete dusted over with gray dust. A dead june bug on its back, legs folded. I wished I was that june bug.

After a while I slid back in the chair and began to rock, staring into the glinting sea of gravel.

Chapter 21
———

Another Week

The new campers arrived that afternoon in a thunderstorm. Most of the kids who were staying over hung around in the dining hall or out on its wide porch, watching as vans and SUVs rumbled in, maneuvering to park as near the building as possible. People leaped from their vehicles and dashed for the porch, loaded with backpacks and sleeping bags, wiping rain from their faces as they came up the steps.

I stayed close to Isabel, and as far from Monica as possible. I'd explained to Isabel about Mama's operation, leaving Monica's existence out of it. But Isabel hadn't forgotten.

She pointed at Monica, leaning against the wall. "Is that girl your sister?"

There was nothing I could do but say yes.

"I thought you said she wasn't at camp." The wide blue eyes were fixed on me.

"Um—I don't think I said that—did I?" I answered, as innocently as I could manage. "Yeah, she was here."

"Oh," Isabel said skeptically, but she let it drop.

Name-tagged counselors with clipboards went around greeting the newcomers and pointing out where they should pile their things. I looked curiously at the ones who seemed to be joining Jeff and Amy's group—a slightly flat-faced boy with red hair, a girl with a lot of well-tanned middle showing between her shorts and her top, and a fat boy in a Nike T-shirt three sizes too big.

In spite of the dismal weather the counselors all acted cheerful. Amy was positively beaming. She was wearing her SMILE — GOD LOVES YOU pin next to her name tag.

A huge lightning flash lit up half the sky, and a second or two later there was a boom so loud it surrounded us—it seemed to come from all directions at once. It made my heart thump, and I shrank back against the wall, even as I told myself I was too old to be afraid of thunder.

Tommy and a couple of other boys whooped and hollered. "Oh baby, that's the best one yet," one of them yelled. Either they actually liked the noise of thunder, I thought, or they were scared and trying to cover it up.

Monica—the dork—seemed to be trying to join in, or maybe just to show she was older than most of us. "Thunder can't hurt you," she said loudly, to nobody in particular. As if we didn't know that, even the third graders, although a couple of them did scurry inside. "It's nothing but air expanding."

"Thanks, professor," said one of the giggling boys, saluting her and squeezing a grin back behind his teeth. "Thanks for telling us." He went back to shoving and fooling around with the others.

"Dummy," Monica muttered.

Dork, dork, dork, I thought grimly, although it also occurred to me that on a basketball court she could show those boys a thing or two. But there wasn't so much as a single hoop at Gilead.

That evening after supper and singing, a steady rain was still falling, so nearly everyone hung around the dining hall, playing games or just talking. I sat alone at a table in the corner, reading a book. I'd found it on the meagerly stocked bookshelf next to the game table, and it was a stupid book, part of some series about a nurse. On the cover was an old-fashioned picture of a nurse in a white dress and a little white cap, looking over the shoulder at a doctor in the background. You could tell he was meant to look handsome, but what he really looked like was an idiot.

Jeff came over and sat beside me.

"Whatcha reading?" he asked.

"Some stupid book," I said, and let it fall onto the table, closed and without a bookmark.

"This is all kind of a shock, huh?" he said, crossing an ankle over the other knee. "I mean, like, you were expecting to go home today, and instead you find out your mom's sick and you have to stay another week."

"Yeah." I stared out across the crowded, noisy dining hall. Isabel was playing Monopoly with some other kids, and Monica was watching. Amy and a couple of other counselors sat talking at one of the tables. Tommy and Kevin were trying to juggle tennis balls. On the far side of the room a girl who looked about eight was pounding out "Heart and Soul" on the plinkety old piano.

"Did you get to talk to your dad?"

"Yeah. They knew all along that she had to have this operation. They just didn't tell us." I could hear the bitter edge in my voice.

Jeff had a puzzled frown, so I explained. "She was supposed to have the operation Friday and be back home before we got home from camp. But a couple of emergencies came up that the doctor had to take care of, so he put off her operation till next Wednesday. So Daddy called Mr. Haywood and asked him if we could stay here another week."

Jeff nodded. "So you're mad that they didn't tell you, and you're probably worried about your mom, too."

"Yeah. I mean, I'm not *too* worried, because Daddy said it's not dangerous. It's called a hysterectomy, where they have to take out a woman's—uterus?"

Jeff nodded again.

"She's going to have to rest for a long time, but she'll be okay."

"Sure, absolutely."

I felt slightly better, hearing Jeff's calm voice confirming that everything would be fine. But still—home was far away, and I was stuck here with Monica. I scowled across the dining hall.

Jeff was looking at me, I could see from the corner of my eye. He was waiting for me to say something.

"I want to be there and take care of Mama," I burst out. "And I don't want to be stuck here with my stupid sister."

"I bet when you do get home you can still do a lot to help your mom," Jeff said. "But I know what you mean about sisters. I always wanted to get away from my big sister. A big sister can really drive you crazy."

What do you *know*, I thought coldly.

After that I said very little to him or anyone else for the rest of the night, not in the dining hall and not in the cabin, where I hid myself close to the concrete-block wall in one of the top bunks. Isabel was below me. Amy was in another top one, with Monica underneath her, and the new girl, whose name was Jasmine, had a bunk to herself. It was a long time before I slept.

The next morning after breakfast, Tommy poked his head into the girls' side of the cabin. Only Monica and I were there; the others were still in the dining hall. "Hey, Erin."

"Yeah?"

"Guess what I had for breakfast? Seafood!" He opened his mouth wide to reveal a disgusting mess.

"Yuck. As I've said before, Tommy, you are gross, gross, gross."

Monica made a face but said nothing.

He leaned in the doorway, spinning a baseball cap on one finger. "Just trying to cheer you up, Erin. You don't look too thrilled about another week with me and the lovey-birds."

"Who's the lovey-birds?" Monica said.

I didn't even glance her way. "Oh, I'm thrilled all right, Tommy. You bet. I'm happy as a lark."

"The counselors," Tommy explained to Monica. "Jeff and Amy."

"Oh." Monica turned away and started rummaging in her backpack.

"Your mom's gonna be okay, you know," Tommy said. He kept spinning the cap and didn't look at either of us. "I heard Mr. Haywood talking to Jean—you know, the cook? He said it's not that bad of an operation; your dad just wanted you to stay here so you wouldn't be home alone."

"Oh," I said. "Yeah, I know." But I felt a little lighter. "Hey, Tommy. Don't tell the new kids about Jeff and Amy, okay? Let 'em figure it out."

He gave me a grinning thumbs-up and disappeared.

Later, at the very first after-lunch rest time, when we all climbed into our bunks, Monica took something out of her backpack that I'd never suspected she had brought—her knitting. I groaned silently, my insides clenching. Further evidence of her dorkiness—as if Isabel and Jasmine hadn't already pegged her as a dork because of her baggy T-shirts and too-long shorts, her unshaved legs, the way she hardly talked to anybody.

She must have been working on her knitting project during the past week, because whatever it was had gotten bigger. She sat on the edge of her bed with a tumble of heathery green yarn in her lap, and the two big needles began to click.

Good old Grandma Monica. I rolled onto my back and clapped my pillow over my face. I wondered if someone would snicker, or if they'd just roll their eyes.

With my nose in the faintly damp cotton pillowcase, I listened as Jasmine and Isabel continued talking about a movie they'd seen. It didn't sound like anyone was paying attention to Monica.

Then Jasmine, who so far hadn't worn a single item of clothing without an expensive label showing, suddenly said, "Hey, Monica, what are you making?"

"Huh? Oh, just a sweater."

I was surprised, never having seen her knit anything more complicated than a plain scarf. But I was even more surprised at what came next.

"That is so cool," Jasmine said, and then Isabel said,

"Let me see." I pushed aside the pillow and looked down in time to see her hop off her bed and go over to look at Monica's knitting.

"My cousin just taught me how to knit," Isabel said. "But I haven't made anything that hard yet. But my cousin, she's so great at it—she made this beautiful red sweater for her mom last Christmas."

Amy looked down from the bunk above Monica. "Monica, you're so talented! Wish I knew how to knit."

Monica seemed flustered by all the attention. "Oh," she murmured, "well, I don't know. I—I've never tried a sweater before."

"I totally, totally *love* that color," Jasmine said.

I lay there staring at the ceiling. My stomach was relaxing, now that Monica's knitting hadn't embarrassed me after all. On the other hand, I'd always thought knitting was old-lady stuff—so when did it get to be cool, and why didn't I know about it?

Even if knitting *was* cool, it couldn't make up for Monica being Monica.

Chapter 22

In the Same Boat

"Erin, how come you hate me?"

This came totally out of nowhere, from behind my back, after a long silence. It was Tuesday afternoon. Monica and I were in a canoe on the lake, and she was in the stern while I sat in the bow, paddling halfheartedly and staring at the forest that came right down to the edge of the water. We were supposed to be aiming for the far side of the lake, opposite to the swimming area and dock. But Jeff had told us to take our time, explore a little, practice maneuvering. Now the green and yellow and red fiberglass canoes were scattered over the lake, and there was no one else close enough to hear what Monica said.

The silence had been grim, at least on my side. Isabel and Jasmine had quickly paired up—I wondered if Isabel liked me less now that Monica had joined us—and so had the counselors and the four boys, leaving me no one to canoe with except Monica. It wasn't fair. I wanted to get away from her, not get trapped in a canoe with her.

"Who says I hate you?" I answered without turning around.

"Well, you act like it."

When I didn't answer, she went on. "You think it's my fault that you got caught for cutting Kayla's hair."

This time I did turn and look at her, letting my paddle drag in the water. "Well, it *is* your fault. And you ruined practically my whole summer."

She laid her paddle across her knees and glared back at me. "I didn't *mean* to get you in trouble. I didn't know Mama was going to walk in right then."

My answer came out in a rush. "Yeah, well, that's just the kind of dorky thing you always do. You say the wrong thing at the wrong time. You wear weird clothes. You—"

"I didn't mean to, okay?" she interrupted hotly. "I'm *sorry*. I'm sorry you got caught."

Still half turned, my paddle now lying across the bow, I stared down at the water alongside the canoe. Under a hazy sky the lake water was light green today, gleaming but murky; looking into it was like looking through an old glass bottle. Out here it was fifty feet deep, Jeff had said. My eyes caught a flicker that must have been a fish, and then it was gone.

We drifted, the water sloshing faintly against the dark green fiberglass of the canoe.

I heard Monica take a deep breath. "Anyway, you already hated me, didn't you? You hated me even before that happened. You think I'm such a dork, you don't even want to go to the same school as me."

I wondered how she knew that. I shrugged uncomfortably, then risked a glance at her. Would she start crying, or hit me with the paddle, or—?

She did neither. "Well, guess what, Erin?" She separated her words as if punching each one of them: "I'm just the way I am." She stabbed her paddle into the water. "Come on—paddle."

I watched her angry, splattery strokes for a moment, and then I started paddling too. We headed straight for the other side.

In bed that night, in my slightly musty, plaid-lined sleeping bag, I shifted every which way, annoyed by each rustle of the bag and creak of the bed frame yet unable to keep still. I kept thinking of Monica saying, "How come you hate me?" and "You don't even want to go to the same school as me." I had said a lot of not-so-nice things to her, but I'd never said I hated her or that I dreaded being in the same school. It was unsettling to find out that somehow she knew. Not only knew but was hurt by it.

And there was something else she'd said in the canoe—for the first time she had apologized for letting Mama know

I'd gone out that night. She hadn't thought Mama would hear, had never intended for her to hear. Somewhere in the back of my mind, I realized, I'd known that all along. Of course it was an accident. Monica might be a dork but she wasn't mean. Bossy, yes, but a tattletale, someone who liked to get other people in trouble? That wasn't Monica.

Once again I rolled from my back to my side without finding a comfortable position. I winced, one eye scrunching into the pillow, and made myself hold still. In the dark cabin only an occasional sigh revealed the presence of other people. Outside, the sounds of a summer night in the mountains drowned themselves in the cicadas' mindless, monotonous chorus.

I'd focused all the blame for the miserable aftermath of my nighttime adventure on Monica. But her role in the whole thing had been accidental. If I was going to hand out blame, I'd have to pin it on someone else.

The next day, Wednesday, was the day of Mama's operation. I thought about it a lot—at canoe practice, while Jeff was demonstrating the J-stroke; in the dining hall, while Reverend Haywood said a too-long grace before lunch; during quiet time, while I lay in my bunk and tried to read a book. It was creepy to think about—Mama lying on a table unconscious, being cut open with a knife, and part of her insides being taken out. The thought of it nagged at me.

After quiet time our group straggled toward the craft house, where we were supposed to paint the birdhouses we'd hammered together the day before. As we followed the gravel path behind the dining hall, for once I didn't avoid Monica. I hurried to get beside her and looked up, suddenly aware of how much taller she was than me. Her face, behind the big owlish glasses, wore one of her stubborn silent looks.

"Hey, Monica."

She glanced down at me, then looked away. "What?"

"Do you think Mama's gonna be okay?"

"Sure she is."

"How do you know?"

She shrugged. "I just know."

I didn't feel especially reassured. I knew that stubborn look much too well. There might be no reason at all for what she said, and if there was one, she wasn't about to explain it. On the other hand—I surprised myself with this idea—maybe her stubborn look was really a worried look. Maybe now, and even some other times when she acted like this, she wasn't just pigheaded but worried or scared.

"Well, I wish Daddy would call us," I said, scuffing through the gravel. "Maybe the operation's already over."

"It's not. It's not supposed to start till two o'clock."

"How do you know *that*?"

"Daddy told me when it was my turn on the phone."

"Oh." I considered, with annoyance, the fact that he hadn't told me this detail. "Well, if he doesn't call this afternoon, I'm going to call him."

"Not till five o'clock. I already asked Mr. Haywood if we could come to the office then and call."

I was surprised that she'd taken the initiative, but I didn't have a chance to say that or anything else. As if to prevent an answer, she abruptly stepped ahead of me and away down the path with her long strides. In a moment we were filing up the three stone steps into the craft house.

It was just one room, nearly filled by two large tables with stools scattered around them. At the far end were shelves overflowing with supplies—paint, wood, pipe cleaners, cardboard, wire, scissors, glue, beads, Popsicle sticks, you name it. There was one big window on each side, with screens but no glass. The air in the craft house had the earthy smell of the woods, with a hint of paint thrown in.

The ten of us jostled our way in, each claiming a stool and workspace at one of the tables. The craft counselor, a middle-aged, hawk-nosed woman named Marta, handed out our birdhouses, calling out the names we'd penciled on the bottom.

"Where's my turd house?" Tommy said, elaborately craning his neck and looking all around. "Gotta paint my turd house."

The boys laughed, Isabel rolled her eyes, Marta pretended not to hear.

"You gonna paint it *browwnn*?" drawled Zach, the really fat kid. Howls from the boys.

I didn't have much to say, just started painting, half listening to scattered bits of conversation. Jasmine was talking about how her brother made a birdhouse once and their kitten slept in it. Isabel pointed to a jar of red paint and said,

"That's the color I want on my nails." The flat-faced boy, Leo, said, "If you paint it blue, will you get bluebirds? Or blue turds?"

As I brushed pink paint on the sides of my birdhouse and yellow on its roof, I thought of Mama lying very still on the operating table, surrounded by people in green masks and gowns. I thought of how far away she and Daddy were, at the hospital in New Bern. To be sitting here at a newspaper-covered table in a one-room, tin-roofed cabin in the mountains, painting a birdhouse pink and yellow, seemed like about the most useless, pointless thing a person could do.

And yet, at the same time, I felt I needed to paint it perfectly, to fill the long afternoon with precise strokes of the brush, spilling nothing, smoothing the brush lines from the wet surface. Around me everyone else kept laughing and chattering as they painted. Only my sister and I were silent.

I looked over at Monica, who appeared to be concentrating hard on the dark green she was glopping onto her birdhouse. I was glad I wasn't the only one who was quiet. I was glad she had arranged for us to use the phone.

I was even, a tiny bit, glad she was here.

Chapter 23

Mount Franklin

We knocked on the door of the camp office, heard Mr. Haywood say, "Come on in," and stepped into the miraculous chill put out by a whirring air conditioner that blocked most of the single window.

Mr. Haywood pointed out the phone, half hidden under scattered papers on a dirty-gray metal desk, and handed me a piece of paper with the number for Mama's hospital room.

"I'll be back in a little while, girls," Mr. Haywood said. "Make sure you close the door when you leave—gotta keep the cool in."

Monica and I argued about who would make the call until, grudgingly, I let her win.

Daddy answered right away, and even though Monica didn't say a lot, it was easy to tell from her expression and her words that nothing was wrong. After a couple of minutes she handed the phone over to me.

"Hey, Daddy."

"Hey, punkin."

"So Mama's okay?"

"Yep. Kind of groggy from the anesthesia, but the operation went real well." He sounded a little tired but cheerful.

"When does she get to go home?"

"Oh, maybe tomorrow, maybe next day. Have to see how she's feeling. How's camp?"

"Okay. Can I talk to Mama?"

"Well . . ." He spoke away from the phone. "Sue, you up to a conversation?" A moment later I heard a quiet "hello."

"Hi Mama, how are you doing?"

"Oh, I'm all right. . . ." She spoke very slowly, and drifted into silence.

"Mama?" I said anxiously.

"Yes, honey . . . You talk to Daddy now. Love you." I worried through several seconds of bumpy fumbling noises as she handed the phone back to Daddy.

"Is she *really* okay, Daddy? She sounds—I don't know, sick."

"No, she's fine," he answered calmly. "She's just sleepy from all the medicine they gave her to keep her out of pain."

"I wish I hadn't talked to her," I said sulkily, mad that the happy feeling of relief had been dimmed, and wanting someone to baby me.

It surprised me a little that Daddy seemed to understand. "Don't you worry, honey," he said in a comforting voice. "Mama's fine. Next time you see her she'll be wide-awake and give you a big hug."

"I want to come home, Daddy. Can we come home early?" I pleaded.

"Mmm, I don't think so, punkin. Best to let your mama rest and me get some work done, and we'll pick you up on Sunday. Least I will, maybe Mama too, if she feels up to a drive."

"Aww," I whined, but then remembered something. "Guess what? Friday we're going to hike all the way up Mount Franklin and camp out."

I'd never been to Mount Franklin, though I knew it was the highest peak anywhere near Gilead. We were going to drive to a parking area at the base, eat an early lunch, hike all afternoon, and spend the night at a campground near the top. The next day we'd hike down again and drive back to camp.

I told Daddy the whole plan for the trip. The time between now and Sunday, I realized, was going to go flying.

Friday morning we piled into two vans—all four boys in the one Jeff was driving, all four girls in the one with Amy at the wheel. The back sections of both vans were crammed with backpacks, sleeping bags, tents, and food. I didn't see how we were going to carry all that stuff up a mountain, even if we did eat some of the food before we started.

But I wasn't worried about it. As I bounced into the middle seat between Isabel and Jasmine, I felt strong enough to carry just about anything. It was a beautiful sunny day, we were off on an adventure, and Mama was fine.

The chatter of the girls in Amy's van, the hum of the motor, the cozy feeling of traveling with the sun on my legs—all came to a halt with a sudden, rapid *whump whump whump*, from somewhere outside but strangely close to us. As Amy pulled over to the side of the highway, we were all saying, "What's that? What's going on?"

Unbuckling her seat beat, Amy answered, "That's the sweet sound of a flat tire, gang."

One by one we jumped out the big side door of the van and looked at the squashed tire, then gazed around. There wasn't a single house or barn in sight.

Amy stared down the highway, where heat shimmers hovered above the asphalt. "Jeff was right in front of us," she muttered. "You'd think he might have noticed we disappeared."

She tried her cell phone, but it was useless out here.

Very soon it was obvious that Amy had never changed a tire. There were long moments when she stared, frowning, at the directions in the owner's manual.

The rest of us sat on the hillside, fiddling with grass and

clover, plucking the blue petals off chicory blossoms. An occasional car sped past in a wave of sound that gathered
toward us, then whipped past and was gone.

Finally I heard a car slowing and looked up to see Jeff's
van coast by, then do a hard U-turn to pull up behind ours.
All four of us suddenly came to life, cheering and dashing
down the slope to meet the rescuers.

Amy had just managed to get the flat tire off, and Jeff
did the rest. By the time we got going again, we'd lost nearly
an hour.

Besides tire changing, there was something else Amy
had never done, and neither had Jeff: drive from Gilead to
Mount Franklin. A wrong turn on the curving, always rising
back roads cost us almost another hour. By the time we made
it to the small parking area at the base of the mountain, the
early lunch we'd planned had turned into a late one.

We climbed out of the vans into air that was noticeably
cooler. Aside from the gray road and the gravel under our
feet, everything around us was green. But it wasn't all the
same. There was forest green, yellow green, jungle green,
kelly green, gray green—all shifting and rustling in a light
breeze. The woods were alive, waiting for us to plunge in.

Amy and Jeff conferred while we munched on sandwiches and chips. They decided that we could make it to the
top before dark, if we kept up a good pace.

If.

We finished eating, used the Porta Pottis that stood at

one end of the parking area, and put on our backpacks. Most of us had fairly small packs with our sleeping bags tied underneath. But then the counselors started adding things. They strapped tents and cooking pots on people's backpacks. They put boxes of pasta and bags of raisins and peanuts into other packs. Each of us already had a good-size water bottle, so the packs weren't light to begin with. There was some arguing over who was being made to carry too much.

Jasmine winced as Amy strapped a tent onto her pack. "I just don't think I can *do* this. Like, all the way up that mountain? I'm not a *mule*."

"I can handle it," said Leo. He squared his shoulders and stepped briskly up to Amy like a soldier volunteering for hazardous duty. "No problem. Just put it on me." With a shrug Amy took the tent off Jasmine and attached it to Leo's pack, which already held a lot of food.

Jeff paced around with his pack on, snapping his fingers. "Come on, come on, let's move."

Finally we were off, with Tommy singing, "A mule is an animal with long funny ears, he kicks up at everything he hears."

For a while everything went well. Walking felt good after a morning in the van, and the trail was pretty, with wildflowers all around and the familiar, earthy smell of the woods. When we stopped for a rest and a drink from our water bottles, Jeff said we were making good time.

Later, though, I caught up with the leaders, sitting on a

long, half-rotten log beside the path. "I thought we might be getting too spread out," Amy said when I asked what was going on. "We're waiting for the rest of the group."

Isabel soon came up behind me, and I counted: seven of the ten of us were there. It must have been ten or fifteen more minutes before the last three caught up.

Zach was panting, his heavy body dripping sweat. He was obviously not in shape for a climb like this. Jasmine looked really tired. Jeff, it turned out, was carrying much of her load.

We stayed there awhile longer so the stragglers could rest, then moved on, all of us slower than before.

An hour later we stopped for the third time. The sun was low and orange. Jeff and Amy weren't sure how far we were from the top. "Can't be more than an hour, even at this pace," Jeff said.

"It'll be dark before we get there," Amy said, "but I don't see anywhere to camp around here. The woods are so dense."

"Setting up camp in the dark. Oh yeah, I love it," Jeff said. "Let's get going."

The word *dusk* had always made me think of *dust* and *hush*, but never so much as it did that day. On the way up Mount Franklin, dusk filtered in among us like a fine powdery dust, blurring my vision, ever so slightly at first, then more and more. I had to look hard at the trail to avoid tripping on rocks and roots. When I glanced up, there was Leo walking in front of me, as he had been for the last half hour, but I couldn't be sure anymore whether it was Isabel or Jasmine in front of him.

There were no voices to give me a clue. We were all tired, too tired to talk, except for Tommy and Amy, who were in the lead; now and then their voices drifted back to me. The only other sounds came from crickets and mosquitoes and footsteps—soft thumps on dirt and the occasional scrape of a shoe on rocks.

An oddly shaped tree or boulder, a matted clump of laurel, the exposed roots of a fallen tree began to look scary. I thought of the mysterious forests of *The Lord of the Rings*. There was the Old Forest, where the shrubs and trees somehow steered the hobbits off their course and toward the evil willow that would trap them. There was Fangorn, dense and smothering. But Frodo and his friends were all right, protected in the Old Forest by Tom Bombadil, in Fangorn by the treelike Ents.

I began pretending to be Frodo, heading safely out of the forest under the care of Tom Bombadil. It was good to think of Tom's huge energy and kindness, and the funny way his talk and his singing ran together. On the rough trail my feet would be as sure as a hobbit's, and . . .

It was no use. I couldn't think myself into the dream of being Frodo. But not because my thoughts were overwhelmed by the real world pushing in, poking holes in the dream. That had happened lots of times before, like when Mrs. Winsted caught me dreaming and told me to sit down. This was something different. This was myself interfering. Pretending just didn't feel satisfying or interesting enough for me to lose myself in it. I was, I realized suddenly, too old for it.

In fact, I hadn't done it in a long time. Hardly ever since the night I cut Kayla's hair. That night I hadn't just changed someone's hairstyle; I'd changed my whole summer. Maybe even my whole self.

Ever so slowly at first, then faster, the dusk deepened, colors faded, shapes wavered and blended into one another. The sun was long gone, but the sky still held a little of its light, so the first stars shone against indigo, not yet black. There was a sliver of moon, too thin to light our way.

Most of us had our flashlights out, though the counselors warned us to use them sparingly; we'd need them to find firewood, cook, eat, and set up tents. The solid barrel of mine, with its heavy D batteries, felt good in my hand. I kept a finger on the switch.

We hiked in a tighter group now, not so strung out along the trail. We were all tired and hungry, but I heard only a few complaints, and they were spoken quietly, as though our voices had dimmed along with the light. Even Tommy, who had hardly stopped yakking and singing all day, had gone silent, somewhere up in front.

I kept in the middle of the group, again behind Leo, and tried not to think about the little boy who was lost in the laurel hells and never found. But it was hard not to think of him, with laurel and twining honeysuckle and leathery rhododendron surrounding us. The shrubs were dense even by daylight, and now the dark blurred and packed them into solid, impenetrable mounds.

Anything could be hidden in there. Branches leaned over the trail as if to snare me. I jumped when my arm brushed one I hadn't seen. The shapes of the bushes could look like a bear or a crouching man, but I was afraid even when they looked like nothing but bushes. What would that little boy have felt, with night coming on, no parents near, and no way out of the laurel maze?

And so, when something large leaped from the bushes onto the trail right in front of me, I was primed to scream, and the sound out of my mouth was like nothing I'd ever heard before.

Chapter 24

Night

The creature gave a weird groaning scream of its own. From up and down the trail came shouts and waving light beams. I clicked my flashlight on and saw that the creature was Tommy.

"Tommy, I'll—I'll *kill* you—I'll *strangle* you. That was not funny!" I yelled.

But Tommy wasn't laughing, and he wasn't getting up from where he'd landed in a heap. He was moaning and holding his ankle. "I think I broke it," he croaked.

In a minute the whole group had gathered around, as close as they could on the narrow trail. The counselors examined the ankle and said it might be broken, they weren't sure. After a few minutes they got Tommy up on one foot, but even with Jeff holding him, he couldn't take a single hop without a cry of pain.

With a sigh Jeff lowered Tommy so he could sit on the ground again.

"Now what?" Amy said to Jeff. "We can't camp here. We can't take him up to the top and then bring him all the way down tomorrow. I'm thinking we've got to take him down tonight."

"Well, what are the options?" said Jeff. "I agree, it would be stupid to take him up and then down tomorrow. Camping here's not impossible. . . ." He looked around, and so did the rest of us. The only way I could imagine camping here was by laying our sleeping bags end to end down the trail. And it was a steep, rocky stretch of the trail, and much too narrow to set up tents.

"Scratch that," Jeff said. "It's impossible."

Amy shrugged off her pack and let it slide to the ground. "So is taking this whole tired crew back down in the dark. We'd have about five more busted ankles." For a moment she pressed a hand to her forehead, as if her head ached. "How about we sit here a few minutes, have a snack, and figure out who goes up and who goes down?"

It didn't take Jeff and Amy long to make their plan. Clearly a counselor had to stay with the main group. Jeff, being stronger, should be the one to help carry Tommy. As for who would take the other end of the stretcher, Monica, as the tallest, oldest, and probably strongest of the campers, was the logical choice. Jeff told her, and she nodded. "Sure. I can do it."

"Oh cheese, I'm ruining everybody's trip," muttered Tommy. He was sitting on the ground with his foot propped up on his backpack. The ankle looked swollen, and his face was tight with pain.

"You're not ruining anybody's trip," Amy said, patting his arm. "Just testing our ingenuity." She shook her head. "Wish we had some ice for that."

Two other campers, the counselors decided, would be needed to carry flashlights and to relieve the stretcher bearers occasionally. Tommy was smaller than most of the other kids, but still, carrying him that far was going to be tough. Amy and Jeff were silent for a moment, looking around the group.

I was sitting on my rolled-up sleeping bag next to Amy, eating an apple and listening. This was something I hadn't thought of. Should I volunteer? Despite the darkness, I didn't want to miss camping at the top of the mountain. But Tommy and his carriers needed help, and with them I could do something important; I could go like Sam and Frodo into the darkness of Mordor.

Even if I couldn't pretend to *be* Sam or Frodo anymore, I could pretend to be as brave as they were.

Jeff and Amy whispered together, and then Amy said, "Leo? Think you could go down with Jeff and Monica— carry a flashlight for them, and maybe take one end of the stretcher now and then?"

"Yeah," said Leo, extremely offhanded. "No problem." You could tell he was trying very hard to sound manly.

"Thanks, Leo," Jeff smiled.

Before they could call on anyone else, I blurted out, "I want to go too."

The counselors looked mildly surprised, but after a quick glance at each other they nodded. "Okay, Erin," Jeff said. "You're on the team."

A lot of gear had to be rearranged after that. Amy and Jeff made a stretcher out of tent poles and a ground cloth, then spread Tommy's sleeping bag on it. Amy tied the remainder of that tent onto her own pack. Those of us who were going down gave the others everything big that we wouldn't be using—tents, cooking pots, food. We kept our own packs and sleeping bags, our water bottles, and some peanuts and raisins. Leo insisted on carrying Tommy's pack as well as his own, managing to lengthen the straps on one so that it would fit on top of the other.

A few minutes later, with Amy like a shepherd at the end of the line, the other half of the group headed up the trail and vanished around a curve. Jeff, Monica, Tommy, Leo, and I began creeping down the mountain. It was really and truly night.

Leo led the way with a flashlight in each hand, one aimed at the trail ahead, one pointing slightly behind him to help Jeff, who held the front end of the stretcher. Monica carried the back end, near Tommy's feet, and I walked behind her, trying to keep my light aimed in front of her.

"Ah, this is the life," said Tommy, hands folded on his chest. "The only way to travel." But the stretcher jostled over a bumpy section of trail, and he gave a smothered groan.

A little later he began singing "I got a mule and her name is Sal, fifteen miles on the Erie Canal. Looow bridge, everybody down." Jeff joined in, but the rest of us kept quiet, listening to their voices sailing out into the black night, our eyes on the flashlight beams and our stumbling feet.

After a while the singing died out and nobody said anything.

Time passed very, very slowly. There were no landmarks, nothing I could remember passing on the way up, nothing recognizable in the dark. The woods around us were solid black, the trail before us nearly black, the darkness relieved only slightly by stars and the little scrap of moon.

I stared at the circle my flashlight made, keeping it in front of Monica's feet. If I wasn't constantly vigilant, she could trip, maybe hurting herself and Tommy too. There wasn't room enough for us to walk side by side, so I was almost directly behind her. The light had to be for her, and so I stumbled sometimes as I stepped into blackness, trying to avoid the rocks and roots I'd seen in the circle a moment before.

This took so much concentration, and I stared so hard at the ground, that often I walked right into thin branches hanging over the trail.

In spite of my efforts and Leo's, the stretcher bearers sometimes tripped. "Keep it in front of me, man," Jeff said once or twice.

We stopped for a rest, and then I carried Monica's end for a while. I couldn't do it for long. My hands and shoulders began trembling with the effort. Then Monica took her end again, and Jeff gave his to Leo. And so on, trading places, all down the endless mountain, with Monica and Jeff doing most of the work, Leo and me helping for shorter periods. I was the weakest by far. Maybe I shouldn't have come, I thought; maybe another one of the kids could have done better.

Monica never complained about how I managed the flashlight, or how short a time I carried the stretcher. She hardly opened her mouth, except now and then to ask for a rest. She usually had to be the one to ask, because Jeff was so much stronger than any of us.

"Doing okay, Monica?" he'd call back sometimes.

She would usually say yes.

One of those times, I somehow knew she regretted that *yes* the minute it came out of her mouth. And I knew she wouldn't take it back. Even by the faint light the stars and moon gave, I could see exhaustion in her face, maybe a tremble in her arms. My own feet and legs were aching.

I put my right hand on the tent pole in front of her right hand and grasped it tight. "I'll take it—you take the light," I whispered. She hesitated, then said quietly, "Jeff, stop a second." We traded the stretcher and the flashlight, and moved on.

I thought of Sam and Frodo, and how the job they had to do was not only frightening but just plain *hard*—physically, mentally, hour after hour, day after day, tired cold hungry confused lost. . . . By pretending to be as brave as that, I had an idea, a person might really become a little braver.

Somehow, through that endless blur of hours, of dark and heaviness and stumbling, we brought Tommy down the mountain.

The trail broadened and leveled out. There was a streetlight ahead, shining like a full moon through the trees. It shone over the parking area where the vans waited like two old elephants, side by side, quiet and patient and safe.

Chapter 25

Hannah

Whap whap whap whap. Mama and I sat together on the porch swing, watching Monica practice. The morning was still deliciously cool, and I stretched out my legs, flexing my bare feet, content to do nothing but sit here with Mama. It was good to be home.

Monica had picked up her basketball like a long-lost friend almost as soon as we got home from camp on Sunday afternoon, shooting and dribbling in the airless heat until suppertime, and again after supper till the light began to fade. She'd played Monday afternoon, and again Monday evening with Russell Lovinger. Now here she was at it again, nine o'clock Tuesday morning. Nine was the earliest

Mama would let her practice, for fear of disturbing some late-sleeping neighbor.

We'd sat here long enough, Mama and I, to watch half the neighborhood leaving. Mr. and Mrs. Lovinger had driven off together to their construction business. Mr. Blevins had purred away in his Lexus to the grocery store he managed (at least once a week Daddy wondered out loud how a man in his line of work could afford a Lexus), and Mrs. Blevins was out in her straw hat watering their vegetable garden.

Mrs. Pate, who didn't have a husband but did have two little daughters, one in preschool and one in kindergarten, had buckled the girls into their car seats in her pink Jeep and roared out of the driveway, probably late for getting them to day care and herself to work at the Broadway Salon. Daddy had left before any of them.

The *whap* of the ball on pavement and the crash-rattle of the backboard and rim had to be disturbing Gary and Russell. In the summer you might see Russell out around ten or so, but you never saw Gary before noon. Anyway, I thought Russell might not mind the noise too much; he'd seemed really happy to get into a game with Monica last night.

After a day and a half at home, I still hadn't seen or spoken to anyone from my class. Sunday we'd just unpacked and hung around with Mama and Daddy. On Monday Monica and I were both still a little tired. We'd sat around in our pajamas all morning, then made tuna sandwiches for lunch so Mama wouldn't have to.

Just as Daddy had promised, Mama was her old self again, only she needed to rest a lot. She played Uno with us after lunch before going to take a nap. Then the house was really quiet. Daddy was at work, of course, and Monica was either playing basketball or doing something on the computer. I thought I might like to call a friend. But who *were* my friends?

Most of the girls I used to play with were Kayla's friends now, and therefore they couldn't possibly be mine. I'd have to wait awhile to see how they felt about me now—the first day of school was Monday, a week away.

It would be fun to talk to some of the boys, like Jesse Miller and Ricky Talmadge and Sam Lyons. They were so funny, so different from girls. Some of us used to steal Ricky's baseball cap and play keep-away with it, and he'd roar and race after us. He called me "Scissors" sometimes, but he wasn't being mean. The boys didn't care who was on Kayla's side and who wasn't.

But of course I wasn't going to pick up the phone and call a boy.

That left Hannah. I wanted to see her, and at the same time I didn't. I almost wanted to call her, but even more I wanted *her* to call *me*. She knew I was home; Mama had told me that she'd seen Hannah and her mother at the grocery store on Saturday and had told them I'd be home the next day.

All Monday afternoon I fooled around, reading a little, making a house of cards, watching Monica's computer game. I went outside and threw a gray-green, slobbery old tennis ball for Bruce to fetch again and again. All afternoon the phone refused to ring.

On Monday evening after supper Daddy went out to the front yard to start cutting the grass, and Mama went to her vegetable garden in the back. Sometimes on a nice evening she'd putter around there for the longest time, just picking a couple of tomatoes, pulling a few weeds, seeing how big the zucchinis had grown, sometimes stroking the smooth green skin of a bell pepper as if it were a polished gem.

It seemed pretty boring to me, watching her from my bedroom window, but she looked happy and peaceful as she moved slowly from plant to plant.

Restless, I put away the clean clothes Mama had left on my bed, then wandered through the house. Monica was in the living room watching TV. In the kitchen the dishwasher was humming. I turned back toward my room, then on impulse entered Monica's instead.

I paused in the doorway, listening to the guinea pigs rustling around in their box. The room was neater than I expected; unlike me, Monica seemed to have put away everything from camp. On her desk, carefully stacked, were several spiral notebooks and a shrink-wrapped packet of lined paper, with pens and pencils and a sharpener on top. A new three-ring binder lay to the side of them. Her bed with its light summer bedspread was rumpled but more or less made up. I noticed that something stuck out slightly from under the pillow. Curious, I stepped carefully around the guinea pigs and pulled it out.

It was a book, and on the cover was an all-over pattern of roses like old-fashioned wallpaper. Across the roses was a single word, in flowing gold letters: *Diary.*

Amazing. *Monica* kept a diary? I'd always thought diaries were for girls like Laura McLaren—girls with talent and big dreams, and especially girls that boys liked, girls who could flirt with the best-looking boys and snub the rest, girls with a busy, gossipy social life.

But of course Monica, too, was entitled to dreams. . . .

For a moment I was back in Laura's bedroom, wavering as Hannah held up her sister's diary in triumph. Then I slid the book back under Monica's pillow, exactly the way it had been, and left the room.

As I sat in the swing with Mama on Tuesday morning, the thought of Hannah was the one thing that spoiled my contentment.

I tucked my feet up under me and turned toward Mama. There were little gray streaks in her dark hair, which hung to her shoulders, not yet pinned up for the midday heat. She was watching Monica, nodding as the ball swished through the net.

"Mama? What did Hannah say when you saw her at Food Lion? Did she say she'd call me?"

"Well, let me see. I don't think she said that exactly, but she asked when you were getting back and I told her."

"Oh."

Mama's eyes went back to Monica, but when I said nothing more she turned and studied my face. "Well?"

I looked down at my knees and brushed off a speck of dirt. "Well what?" I answered without looking up.

"If you want to talk to Hannah, why don't you call her?"

I shrugged. I wasn't quite sure of the answer, even if I had wanted to explain.

Mama just nodded slowly, gazing at me.

I felt myself flush, irritated by her knowing look. I almost demanded to know what she was nodding about. Then I caught myself, deciding I didn't want to hear.

I faced the basket and tried to look absorbed in Monica's shooting, though I felt Mama's eyes on me.

After a minute Mama went inside to make more coffee. I picked up a couple of magazines that I'd brought out earlier and turned the pages slowly, trying to find something to get interested in. I was staring at sharks in *National Geographic* when the whiz of bike tires made me look up. Hannah was coming up the driveway.

She jumped off and laid the bike on its side in the grass. "Hey," she said, sitting down on the porch steps.

"Well, hey." We looked at each other and looked away.

There was something wary about both of us. It reminded me of Bruce when he met a new dog, and he stopped a little ways off, totally alert, and his whole body quivered, as though he wanted to growl as much as wag his tail, and he wanted to run away as much as either.

Finally Hannah said, "How was camp?"

"Pretty good. But I was ready to come home." I laid the magazine aside. "How was California?"

"Great. Well, almost great. If I could have, like, gone with some friends instead of my family, it would have been really great." She took off her bike helmet and pushed back her hair, then looked me in the eye. "You never answered my e-mail."

"Oh. Well, there wasn't anything to say." I tried to keep my voice neutral. "Except that I was totally grounded and everybody thought I was crazy. I couldn't write about that because your mother might read it."

"Yeah, but I didn't know you got caught until we got home."

I said nothing, and after a minute Hannah said, "You didn't tell on me. You didn't tell anybody, right?"

"Right."

"Thanks, Erin. I mean, that was so nice of you."

I shrugged. "I didn't want to be a rat."

She smiled. "Get your bike. I want to take you somewhere."

"Where?"

"Just somewhere. Come on, tell your mom and let's go."

In the kitchen, I told Mama I was going for a bike ride with Hannah. "I know," Mama said, pouring herself some coffee. "She called a while ago to make sure you were here. She seems to have some mysterious plan."

"Plan?"

Mama just shrugged. "Don't forget your helmet."

Hannah took us in circles, all over Shipley. We passed her house, our old school, the grocery store, Samantha's house. We were riding along a shady street lined with big houses when all of a sudden Hannah braked and turned, right into Kayla Morton's driveway.

I braked, too, but I didn't turn in. "What are you *doing*?" I said in a panic.

Hannah just got off her bike and beckoned to me. She had that daring, do-anything look on her face, and I thought, *Oh no, get away from me, Hannah McLaren.*

But then she looked at me seriously, and I felt that this time she saw *me*, not just her own scheme. "It's okay, Erin. Really. I won't get you in trouble. All you have to do is watch."

Slowly I walked my bike down the driveway and leaned it against a thick shrub. We both took off our helmets, and I followed Hannah to Kayla's front door, the same door where I'd stood and apologized on the most miserable day of my life.

Hannah rang the doorbell, and Kayla herself answered.

"Hi, Kayla," Hannah said cheerfully.

"Hi," she said, but she stared distrustfully at me as I hung back, a good ten feet behind Hannah. Then she looked at Hannah and said, "My mom said you called. She said you wanted to bring me something."

"I did," Hannah answered. "An apology." She took a breath. "Kayla, cutting your hair off was my idea, not Erin's. She wouldn't have done it if it weren't for me. And I'm really sorry. It was a mean, stupid idea."

Kayla looked stunned.

Hannah turned, glancing from me to Kayla and back. "And I want Erin to know that I'm sorry she got all the blame. I should have gotten just as much. Maybe more."

Kayla fiddled nervously with her gold necklace, opened her mouth, then closed it.

"Well, I'm the one who actually did it," I said slowly. "I could have said no to Hannah's idea."

I was about to say more, but Kayla burst out. "It was so horrible. How could you do something like that? How could you be so mean—both of you?"

I forced myself to look straight at Kayla, at the tears of outrage in her eyes. "I'm really sorry, Kayla. I had to say that before, because my mother and your parents were standing here. Now I don't have to. But I *am* sorry."

Kayla sniffed. "It was really really awful." She turned, glancing at her reflection in the glass of the open door, and fluffed out her hair. It was still that gorgeous golden color.

"My mother took me to the best salon in Raleigh," she

said. "Anyway . . ." She gave her reflection another lingering gaze. "I think this cut makes me look more . . . sophisticated."

"Oh yes, definitely," Hannah answered enthusiastically. As well as I knew her, I still couldn't quite tell if she meant it or if she was mocking Kayla's vanity.

"We're gonna go ride some more now," Hannah said.

"Okay," said Kayla.

"Bye," Hannah and I both said.

We got on our bikes and pedaled out of there fast.

Chapter 26

Happy New Year

School. I woke up early on the first day, blinking my way out of some vague, uneasy dream, and then the word *school* plunged to the bottom of my stomach like a rock dropped in a cold pond.

Not just school, but J. B. Marsh Middle School.

First thing, I went to my dresser and took out my best pair of shorts. I looked through a drawer of T-shirts; I pawed through the clothes on hangers in the closet. I wished I had something really cool to wear on the first day.

Hanging in the closet was the slinky purple top I'd bought at the mall, that day I went with Hannah. Mama had said I absolutely could not wear it to school. Fingering the smooth fabric, I sighed. I still thought it was great. Probably lots of other girls would be wearing tops that showed their bellies.

I wondered if Hannah would wear hers, despite her mother's orders—if she would wear a shirt over it, the way she'd said weeks ago, and take off the outside shirt at school. I figured she probably would.

Then I remembered that I'd said I would do it too.

Would I?

I wanted to wear the top just because I liked it. I wanted to wear it to show I was Hannah's friend. But I didn't want trouble with Mama, and I didn't want to sneak around.

I took one more look in the closet and found the answer. I put on the purple top and over it a white shirt with buttons. I tucked the white shirt into my shorts, nice and neat, and looked in the mirror. Purple showed where I'd left the top button open, and purple was dimly visible through the white fabric. I liked the way I looked.

I bounced into Mama and Daddy's room. Mama was getting dressed, and I could hear the scrape of Daddy's razor in the bathroom.

"Mama, can I wear it this way?"

"Good morning to you too."

"Good morning dearest mother queen of the Nile your majesty O mighty one. Can I wear it this way?"

Buttoning her blouse, Mama circled me, studying the outfit from every angle. There was just the slightest frown along her dark eyebrows.

I quivered like a racehorse in the starting gate.

"Yes," she said at last. "Yes, you *may* wear it."

Grinning, I started to dash away.

"*If—*"

"What?" I asked breathlessly.

"If you promise to keep the white shirt on all day."

"I will. I promise!"

Daddy drove us to school, Monica in the front seat and me in the back. It was one of those steamy days—even this early in the morning the air was thick and damp on my skin and in my lungs. I felt nervous and subdued, and kept smoothing my shorts, wishing they weren't so wrinkled. I had a feeling Monica was nervous too.

I stared out the window at familiar sights—the flat, sandy-edged streets, the three blocks of downtown. When we stopped at a red light, I watched Mr. Dean rolling down the clear tinted shade in the front window of his drugstore, and a woman sweeping the sidewalk in front of the flower shop.

It was all familiar and at the same time it was all strange. Partly that was because I'd rarely gone around town so early, seeing people going to work, shops opening up. But it was also because I felt different inside. Every year the first day of school woke up the butterflies in my stomach, and this year I was going to a new school that was about five times as big as my old one. Instead of being in the oldest class in the school, I'd be in the youngest. And to a lot of the kids, I'd be Monica Chaney's little sister.

In no time, it seemed, we were driving up Marsh's long semicircular driveway and stopping at the front door.

"Well, girls," Daddy said, turning toward us as we unbuckled. "Hope you have a fantastic day." He patted Monica's knee and gave me a wink and then we were out on the sidewalk.

As the car pulled away I stared up at the enormous, three-story brick front of the building and the row of six gray doors at the end of the concrete walkway.

"Come on," Monica said, swinging her backpack onto one shoulder. "I'll show you where things are."

"I already know. I had a tour, remember?"

As I followed her to the doors I noticed for the first time what she was wearing—red shorts and a faded orange T-shirt that totally clashed. And, of course, she still hadn't shaved her legs.

I cringed. I almost panicked. I was going to be *seen* with her, seen by everybody with this dork of a sister.

Then I took a deep breath, let it out in a long sigh. Monica was Monica, and she'd never learn how to look cool. She was just the way she was.

Inside, we both stood around nervously, a couple of feet apart. Monica said hi to two kids and briefly compared schedules with one of them. I didn't see anyone I knew, aside from a few eighth graders. To keep from looking friendless, I pretended to be interested in the trophies and ribbons that filled a big glass case along one wall.

Soon the lobby grew crowded and noisy, with kids

milling around, yakking, waiting for the bell that would allow them to go past the lobby, down the long halls to their homerooms. I began to recognize a lot more faces among the strangers.

I talked to Shakara a little—we both had Mrs. Keating for homeroom—and waved to Ricky. Slouching around in his usual baseball cap, he gave me a lazy wave in return, as if this was just any old boring school day. Samantha came through the door, looking as nervous as I'd felt five minutes earlier, and I smiled hesitantly in her direction. She smiled back warmly and said, "Hi, Erin," and even though she didn't come over to me through the crowd, her response felt like a good sign. Like maybe a few of Kayla's friends didn't hate me anymore.

I wished Hannah would get here, but it wouldn't be like her to come early.

Then Kayla herself arrived, with Danielle beside her. Naturally, they stuck together like Siamese twins, gazing around the lobby. Claire, who came in behind her sister, strolled over to a group of girls, probably eighth graders, who were standing right next to me. She wore a short black skirt and a tight, stretchy blue shirt that made her look taller and slimmer than ever.

As she threaded her way through the lobby her glance flickered all around, but she passed by Monica and then me without a word. Just as Claire reached the group, one of them, a short, curly-haired girl, looked over and called, "Hi, Monica."

"Oh, hi, Mariel," I heard Monica answer, and at the same time I heard Claire, with an expression of gleeful disdain, murmur to the group, "Monica just looks so *stylish* today, doesn't she?"

"As always," replied the girl beside her with a giggle.

A glance told me that Monica, farther away than me, hadn't heard. Good. But suddenly I was sick of this kind of thing.

"Hey Claire," I said in a hard voice. "You don't have to be so mean. Just because she doesn't wear cool clothes and stuff." Claire merely looked amused, as though I were a silly little first grader.

I felt myself blushing. I almost said, "Wait till you see her play basketball," but stopped, knowing how childish that would sound to Claire and her friends.

"Okay, Erin," Claire said sweetly, and turned back to her group. And then I was saved by the bell.

Chapter 27

November Games

Laura McLaren drove Hannah and me to school one chilly November night in her mother's minivan. She had just graduated from a learner's permit to a real license, and this was the very first time she'd been allowed to drive after dark. She was so thrilled about driving that she was willing to take Hannah almost anywhere, anytime, and this had done a lot to ease Hannah's resentment of her.

Laura stopped the minivan near the gym entrance. Hannah bounded out of the front seat and shut the door; I slid back the heavy side door, saying thanks to Laura as I stepped out.

"Hannah!" Laura called through the open door.

"Say what?" Hannah said, coming back.

"Remember you're supposed to call home when there's ten minutes left in the game so somebody can pick you up."

"I know, I know, you already told me."

"Do you have change for the phone?"

"Duh. You sound like Mama."

Laura gave a loud sigh. "Shut the door, Hannah. And you're welcome."

"Thank you!" Hannah shouted with a grin as she heaved the door into place.

The gym was bright and noisy, the ceiling lights glaring off the shiny floor, the backboards, the metal railings along the bleachers. There were plenty of places to sit—girls' middle-school basketball doesn't exactly draw huge crowds—but this fall more and more Marsh kids had been showing up, once the word got around that this year's team was stomping every opponent. Boys who used to come only for the later game, the boys', now came early to watch the girls. Mainly to watch Monica.

Hannah and I were right on time; the starting whistle blared as we found seats in the middle of the fourth row. I was a little jumpy, glancing from the game to the spectators, looking to see who had come, feeling mature and on my own without Mama and Daddy. They hadn't missed a single one of Monica's games until now, but tonight there was some church meeting that they thought they should go to.

Whenever there was a break in the action, Monica looked uneasy and awkward on the court. But as soon as she moved, her long limbs somehow flowed in perfect coordination, carrying her down the court and sending the ball up for score after score.

In front of Hannah and me, on the first row, sat the cheerleaders, jumping up to yell and shake pom-poms at every basket. These were all sixth graders; only seventh and eighth graders could be on the varsity squad, which cheered at all the boys' games.

One of the junior cheerleaders was Kayla, and another was Danielle. I figured that was why Samantha came over and sat with us—Kayla and Danielle weren't available. But then Samantha had always been friendlier than they were.

There was a time-out, and we watched the cheerleaders prance through a couple of their routines. When the game resumed, Marsh was already a dozen points ahead of their opponents from Blakesley Middle School, even though it was still the first quarter. From far off to the side Monica scored again, and Kayla whooped, shooting up one pom-pommed hand.

Samantha turned to me. "Isn't it funny? I mean, Kayla used to—well—make fun of Monica. And now she's cheering for her."

"Yeah," I said. "It is kind of funny."

"It's the haircut," said Hannah wickedly. "We trimmed some of the meanness off her."

I caught my breath for a second—Hannah had some nerve, to say that to a friend of Kayla's. But Samantha laughed, really laughed, and then I did too. It was the first time I'd laughed about that whole incident.

When the game was over and we started toward the door, Ricky Talmadge came leaping down the bleachers. "Hey Scissors," he said to me. "Your sister can really play hoops."

"Yeah, I know."

"She used to seem kind of dorky," Ricky said, his voice coming from inside the sweatshirt he was pulling over his head, the eternal baseball cap still on it. His head popped out, the red cap at a slant. "But she's really great."

"She's both," I said. "She's a dork and she's great."

"You got any hidden talents like that?" Ricky asked as we reached the door.

"Nope. I'm not like Monica."

Ricky, Samantha, Hannah, and I jostled our way out into the biting night air. The sky was clear and black behind the haloed streetlights scattered around the walkway and parking lot.

Ricky seemed about to turn away, and quickly I said, "There *is* one talent I've got."

"Yeah, cutting hair!" he grinned.

"No, snatching baseball caps." I plucked it off his head and sent it spinning like a Frisbee into the grass. He raced for it, but Hannah got there first, with Samantha right behind her.

And all around the front lawn of J. B. Marsh Middle School, the four of us had a long, wild game of keep-away under the streetlights, under the enormous velvet sky.